Eeeee
Eee
Eeee

a novel by Tao Lin

MELVILLEHOUSE
BROOKLYN, NEW YORK

© 2007 Tao Lin

Melville House Publishing
145 Plymouth Street
Brooklyn, NY 11201

www.mhpbooks.com
ISBN: 978-1-933633-25-1

Book Design: Kelly Blair

First Melville House Printing: April 2007
Fourth Printing: July 2009

Library of Congress Cataloging-in-Publication Data

Lin, Tao, 1983-
  Eeeee eee eeee / Tao Lin.
     p. cm.
  ISBN-13: 978-1-933633-25-1 (pbk.)
  1. Experimental fiction. I. Title.
  PS3612.I517E35 2007
  813'.6--dc22

                                        2007027513

Printed in the U.S.A.

Andrew talks to Steve on the phone then drives to Domino's. "You're late," Matt says. "You're fired. Get your shit and get the fuck out of here." There are two managers and one is Matt. The other manager is the sad manager.

Andrew grins. "Okay," he says.

Matt stares at Andrew. "I don't want to see you again, Andrew." Matt is twenty-five, singer and guitarist of his own band, and Andrew is making a shit-eating grin at him. Andrew goes to the back, feels tired of life, and logs in. Four other drivers are standing around. Andrew has nothing to say to them. They live in small houses with low roofs and are all very polite. One was a martial arts champion. Andrew had a flat tire once and the martial arts champion drove out to help, late at night. He seemed very nice and a little shy, but also like if he wanted he could walk quietly through a crowd with a neutral facial expression breaking people's bones. Andrew kept apologizing; he felt bad because one time the martial arts champion had showed him how to save fifteen seconds by driving through a field illegally. "Thank you for helping me," Andrew said. The martial arts champion said his wife hit a deer and after that would not drive anymore. He said he used to go places for martial arts competitions. He went to Virginia and Georgia. "I was pretty serious," he said. "I did martial arts one summer," Andrew said. The martial arts champion was changing the tire; they were in front of a rundown grocery shack; and Andrew kept thinking, *martial arts, deer, death*. He was not surprised or afraid, but a little bored. Driving home that night he felt undistracted and grateful. He petted his dogs and emailed his mom. He should be friends with the martial arts champion; with all of them. They once invited Andrew to drink beer and watch TV. *We'll eat pizza.* They laughed when they said that and Andrew smiled and had an image of himself standing in a corner, drunk and depressed, then facedown in a retention pond. At home that night he wondered if he should've gone; imagined it would've been fun, just to watch—the martial arts champion probably would have gotten drunk and jump-kicked a deer, or something—and after that was not invited again.

"Is it busy? Today?" Andrew says. He looks abstractly at the other drivers; it's unfair to look at one person.

"It's been slow this week," someone says.

"Remember when kids said 'slow-mo'?" someone else says. "I'm bringing it back."

"No you're not," Andrew says.

"Why not?"

"I don't know," Andrew says.

The other manager walks by. He is young and overweight, with glasses; 'the sad manager.'

"A moose gave a ten dollar tip," someone says. "I said, 'Thank you, moose.' Moose said, 'Thank you.' It was fun."

When there are no deliveries you fold boxes; or take calls. Folding boxes is easier. Everyone is folding boxes. Andrew is folding boxes. If the entire job were to fold boxes people would scream. They would fold, and sometimes scream, existentially, then be dragged into a field and beaten into a paste. Sometimes there would be a killing rampage. Steve was going to Seattle but got on the wrong plane and is now in New York City. It's risky to scream in an airport. *Steve is clinically depressed inside of an airport, homeless; let him live in your closet. Sara, I'll wear him like a shirt over my head, like a hat, and his ears can be my real ears.*

"My friend was going to see his dad," Andrew says. "He went to New York City."

Someone says something about dying from eating too much pizza after sex with a prostitute.

Andrew feels calm. "If you can't beat them join them," he says. Some days he feels calm. Today he feels calm. He feels strange. "Has anyone done that? Not beaten something... then joined it?"

"If you can't join them buy them out," someone says.

"Buy them presents," Andrew says, and makes a shit-eating grin at no one; at a pizza box. He is embarrassed for the pizza box. He folds it. 'Shit-eating grin.' He needs to stop. He needs to use his face to convey emotions to other humans in order to move sincerely through life—laughing in groups of three or four; expressing gratitude, concern, or disapproval about people, the weather, or food; and manipulating members of either sex to get them to love him, like him, or respect him. That is what a face is for. One manager isn't enough so there are two. They should be identical twins. One would make pizzas shaped like pentagrams and have a pointy tail no one would mention but have nightmares about most nights. Eventually the evil twin would go on a killing rampage, which no one would mention but have nightmares about most nights; though sometimes in daytime, during naps. Everyone is folding boxes. Feels like a David Lynch movie. In Manhattan Andrew saw *Mulholland Drive* with a girl. They saw the movie, ate Chinese food. She kept saying she was having a lot of fun. Andrew liked her. "I really want to do this again," she said at her door. "We should," Andrew said. "I'll call you," she said. Andrew saw her next a few months later, from across a street, and she averted her eyes. Did she avert her eyes? Maybe she was being polite when she said ten times and enthusiastically that she was having a lot of fun. Maybe she was being sarcastic. Maybe politeness is the same as sarcasm. Someone should write that book. *Against Politeness.* Andrew is learning many useful and interesting things while folding boxes for minimum wage. *I was folding boxes and writing a book proposal. My face was neutral but inside I felt productive and good. My name is Andrew. I am twenty-three years old, I live in Orlando, Florida, and instead of talking out loud to real human beings that I can touch and look at I talk in my head to humans from my past that I will probably never see again.*

Matt comes and stares then slowly goes away. Andrew laughs. He likes Matt. If Andrew makes a movie Matt will be in every scene in the background staring. The trailer will be two minutes of Matt's face. One time Matt told Andrew to deliver a pizza with his hat sideways, shirt untucked, belt unbuckled; and gave him a bike chain to wear around his neck. Andrew did it. The man came to the door, terrified. Andrew felt abstract and out-of-control. It took a long time because it was a large order, with Buffalo wings and extra bleu cheese. The man's face turned red and neither of them spoke, even when Andrew dropped a container of bleu cheese and they both watched it fall into a little hole in the concrete. It was difficult to get the bleu cheese out because it fit almost perfectly in the strange hole. "What happened," Matt said. "The person was afraid of me," Andrew said. "You're a good worker," Matt said.

Sitting in the car after work. Listening to music. ("How do you have fun?") Andrew has not spoken aloud in about three hours. He will never speak again. He is ready to go home. He doesn't want to go home. He wants to build a tree fort for Sara. Trap her in the tree fort. Matt comes out, gives Andrew a pizza, says to deliver it to Joanna's house and also drive Joanna home. "Don't rape her, or we'll know," Matt says. Joanna is standing there. "Thank you for the awkward situation," Andrew says. "What?" Matt says. "Thank you for the awkward situation," Andrew says. "What?" Matt says. "Thank you for the awkward situation," Andrew says. Matt lights a cigarette. Joanna stares at Andrew. She waves. Andrew waves. Joanna is four feet from Andrew, who is sitting in his car—a Honda Civic—and they are waving at one another. She is a phone person; a high-schooler. She sits in back. Andrew feels like a chauffer. Matt is training him, taking Domino's to the next level in cutting-edgedness. *Get rid of the tables; introduce chauffeurs.* Andrew drives out of the shopping plaza. He will find Joanna's house without directions. As a boy he was convinced he had extra sensory perception. He read UFO books and was afraid every night. Andrew feels sorry for the small boy who sat in the 'occult' section of shopping-mall bookstores for hours while his mom bought clothes. He is still afraid sometimes that an alien will be standing in a doorway. He wants to fight an alien in hand-to-hand combat, to overcome his fear; aliens would surround him, headbutt him into a paste—it would take six hours, because of their soft heads, but Andrew would be too afraid to object or move—and roll their bodies in the paste. Andrew makes a left. He will not talk unless Joanna talks first. He did that with Sara sometimes. He should talk non-stop and never strategize, or think. People would try to get away from him. Finally the police would take him to jail, though in the morning he would be back, in the person's house, talking loudly. Eventually there would be killing rampages. Eventually there will always be killing rampages.

"Make a right back there," Joanna says. "You were supposed to turn."

U-turn over the median? *You win, you lose, it's the same old news.* Andrew does it. A cop turns his sirens on. "Shit!" Joanna says. She leans forward and looks at Andrew's face. Andrew looks at her. She has a pretty nose, a small mouth. ("Don't rape her, or we'll know.") Andrew looks away, parks the car. If he were Sara he would call the cop a motherfucker. Don't call the cop a motherfucker.

"Tell me what happened," the cop says. He shines a flashlight in back, at Joanna.

"He's giving me a ride home," Joanna says. "I'm in high-school. We're co-workers at Domino's. We just left there."

The flashlight is on Joanna's face; the cop is looking at Andrew. It's a little confusing. 'Complex.'

"I made a U-turn," Andrew says, and makes a kind of shit-eating grin.

"You made a U-turn," the cop says. "Other people got off work and you will kill them— put them in wheelchairs, hospitals. What are you thinking about, boy?" He wasn't angry before. Now he is very angry. He called Andrew a boy.

"I know I'm wrong," Andrew says. He is thinking about marshmallows a little. It is October. "My co-worker's family ordered a pizza." He has an image of himself drunkenly resisting arrest; being shot in the back of the head while running away. He is afraid there are kilograms of illicit drugs in the glove compartment. He will fight the cop in hand-to-hand combat. Don't make sudden movements; not yet. The cop leaves. Andrew promises to himself sarcastically—it is impossible for Andrew to make a sincere or unselfconscious promise to himself—to never make a U-turn again. Not even a legal one. It's good he wasn't wearing a bike chain. The cop returns with a $180 ticket. "Thank you," Andrew says, grinning. He will plead insanity in traffic court. The cop, *He did seem demented.* The judge, *What does it mean that he's grinning right now?* Courtroom psychologist, *Look at that shit-eating grin.* Andrew, *I'm against capitalism, I'm against being against capitalism, and I work at Domino's pizza.* Denny's waitress, *He said I was against capitalism.*

"Should I sit up here?" Joanna says, and climbs up front. "Why did I sit in back? The cop thought that was illegal. He wasn't sure."

As a kid Andrew was always climbing around in cars. His mom liked it. Andrew kind of likes Joanna. Andrew likes Sara. Sara, laughing. Joanna doesn't laugh or smile. Andrew looks at her. Joanna looks at him. Andrew grins a little. Joanna looks away then ahead.

She is afraid. At work she talks nonstop; does she? Andrew never paid attention. He puts on very sarcastic and depressing music. *She used the window instead of using the door /now I'm alone up on the fourteenth floor.* Sarcastic; or polite? Joanna is afraid of this music. Andrew will drive them into a wall. Joanna will make a face of agony. Before they die she will shriek and Andrew will get a headache. The cop will be very angry and shine his flashlight at a tree while talking about the car. Matt will stare, then walk slowly and backwards into a forest. Sara won't ever know. She never thinks about Andrew; hasn't ever e-mailed or called. Andrew never e-mails or calls either, really, just has imaginary conversations with her almost constantly; his idea of her. Maybe he will e-mail her tonight. She will respond with a form letter. *We thank you for your submission but are unable to use your work at this time. Unfortunately, the volume of submissions we receive makes a personal reply impossible.* She'll say she's moving to Florida and Andrew will pet his dogs, e-mail his mom, and buy Steve a present. She won't respond and Andrew will lie on the floor with a blanket over his face and body.

Joanna is saying something.

Andrew turns down the music. He feels bored. "What did you just say?"

"I know this. My sister listens to this. It's I Hate Myself."

"No one listens to I Hate Myself," Andrew says.

"I just said my sister listens to I Hate Myself."

Andrew wants to meet Joanna's sister for dinner.

"I live here," Joanna says.

After eating salads with Joanna's sister they will listen to music and kiss. After eating salads with Joanna's sister they will avert their eyes. To be polite she will swear to God she's having fun, and take a lie detector test. She won't be Sara. Sara is better. Sara didn't listen to I Hate Myself. 'Complex.' 'Shit-eating grin.' Shit-eating grins are complex. Why would you grin if you just ate shit? A neighborhood is passing on the right. Joanna's neighborhood. Andrew in his head has an image of a mouth larger than Andrew's head and the mouth is laughing. Sometimes reading or watching TV Andrew recognizes that a thing is meant to be funny and hears this laughter, in his head, then feels that his face is very calm and neutral, like a hamster's. At night sometimes Andrew's heart beats fast and his thoughts are illogical and wild. In bed he looks at the ceiling and feels excited and alert, and can't understand why he, or anything, exists.

"You passed it," Joanna says. "You passed the first turn too; when we left Domino's. That's why you made a U-turn and got a ticket."

"The first turn you didn't say anything; how could I know?"

"I did," Joanna says.

"I'm pretty sure you didn't."

"I swear I said, 'Turn here, Andrew.'"

"You didn't say my name."

If Joanna were Sara, Andrew would tickle her. He mock jerks the steering wheel to the left. He looks at Joanna. She isn't looking. One time a kid was roadside on a bike and kept glancing over his shoulder as Andrew approached; Andrew mock jerked the car and the kid fell off his bike into a ditch. Sara liked that story. Sara called a guy at Duane Reade a motherfucker. Sara's tongue was very cute, licking her blue Popsicle. Sara Tealsden. Stop thinking about her. Drive Joanna to Joanna's house.

"I'll turn up here," Andrew says. U-turn. Another promise not kept. Of the two people in the car Andrew is the one without a future; the other person, Joanna, will go to college, make myriad friends and life connections, join clubs, get internships, and even marry someone and have children. What was Andrew doing the entire time in college? Everyone was constantly busy and partying, or attempting suicide. Andrew was always telling people how he'd just slept fourteen hours. He joined a water polo club. He had leg cramps and got out of the pool and winced. The instructor said, "You won't be coming back again, will you?" Andrew said,

"Yeah I will." At a deli Andrew saw the instructor and walked up to her and said, "I'll see you next week." He did not go back. He turns the music up, puts it to a different song. Pick a happy one. There are no happy ones. There is no future. It goes to a very depressing song by Samiam. *I don't want to spend another long and lonely weekend by the phone without anyone to call / I've had a lot of time to think and I'm so tired of thinking I know why he put that bullet in his skull.* Sincere, at least. Andrew does not know the meaning of the word 'sincere.' That can't be true. Talk to Joanna. Meet her sister. Kill Joanna, her sister, and Steve. ("Kill me and my siblings.") Suitcase full of cash; high-fives on a diamond boat. Andrew feels sorry for Samiam's singer who is probably currently listening to I Hate Myself. Andrew feels sorry for anything, even inanimate objects and moments in time. He once recorded a song in his room; he feels sorry for those moments in time when a person named Andrew recorded a sad song in his childhood bedroom by dubbing drums with guitar then singing a poem over it. He should put the song on the Internet. Name it "Jhumpa Lahiri." Her Pulitzer Prize would slide into the night and be run over by a car. Sara would laugh. Steve would comprehend that it was funny but not laugh. Joanna probably would not laugh. Joanna's sister, maybe (she listens to I Hate Myself). Matt would stare at Andrew for ten minutes. It's depressing that people are different. Everyone should be one person, who should then kill itself in hand-to-hand combat. The chance that Andrew and Joanna's sister would like one another is probably two percent. Einstein, *God doesn't play dice with the universe.* When Andrew hears something like that his face becomes very neutral and a sarcastic voice in his head says, "Profound." He doesn't want to drive anymore. What will he do tonight? ("Go fuck yourself." "I will. Tonight.") He wants to drive into a mountain and make the mountain explode. Florida has no mountains. Florida has no Sara. No Sara; no future. No marshmallows. Andrew stops thinking.

"You passed where you said you would turn," Joanna says after a while.

"I'll turn soon." Andrew drives thinking, *turn at the next one. I will turn at the next one. Mass grave in the side yard.* He merges smoothly into the turn lane. ("Tell me what happened." "I made a fucking U-turn.") "I'm obsessed with a girl," he says. "What should I do?"

"You're not obsessed," Joanna says.

"She is Sara. She doesn't call me. I made her admit she liked me. She likes me. But we're too alike. When you're with someone and neither of you can stop saying good things. Then you both get very aware that life will end soon. I think that's why we don't talk that much. Do you understand what I'm talking about?"

"You're rationalizing," Joanna says.

Andrew drives without thinking.

He feels calm. He feels a little good.

("My sister is more depressed than both of us.")

"Are you passive-aggressive?" Joanna says. "You don't call but expect her to, like she's your mom."

"She's not my mom." Andrew's mom is in Germany. Steve's mom's plane crashed. "I

don't know what 'passive-aggressive' means.
It's a cliché," Andrew says. He feels tired. What
will he do for the rest of his life? "How old is
your sister?"

"My best friend's cousin's name is Sara,"
Joanna says.

Best friend's cousin. "I can't process what
you just said," Andrew says. Steve's dad,
screaming. "Sara," Andrew says. Everyone
should be named Sara. Rename the dogs.
Interpret them as one entity. 'Sara.'

"Maybe I know her," Joanna says. "I
think three of her cousins are named Sara.
Turn left." She points at her neighborhood;
'Windy Brook.' Andrew has an image of himself and Sara sitting by a stream with their feet
in the water.

"My sister's twenty-five," Joanna says.
"Why?"

Andrew turns into 'Windy Brook.' "Your
sister should start a band with me. My friend
Steve and I are starting a band." Andrew will
marry Joanna's sister. Steve will feel left out.
Killing-rampage.

"Ashley plays bass guitar," Joanna says. "She's okay at it. I mean really good. I'm not jealous; I don't know why I said she's okay. She's great."

"Everyone should be named Sara." A bear with a hose on 'full-blast' setting, watering flower plants—crushing them, really—stares at Andrew's face as Andrew drives by. Andrew thinks about squinting or something and blankly stares back at the bear.

"My sister is a genius on bass guitar," Joanna says, and gives some more directions.

"I feel like how Honda Civics look. That's why I drive a Honda Civic," Andrew says. "Just kidding." He wants Ashley's phone number. *Can I come inside to 'court' your sister?* Inappropriate. Be patient. Wait ten days; don't strategize. Wait exactly fourteen days, get her email address under the pretense of starting a band; use the email address to get her phone number; use the phone number to ask her to dinner under the pretense of something else. Wait fourteen days then go on a killing-rampage, culminating in Seattle with putt-putt, in the rain, with Steve's dad's severed arm. She's twenty-five. Probably in Uzbekistan for the Peace Corps. Andrew is twenty-three. He should join the Peace Corps. He and Sara were going to vacation on the Canary Islands. Andrew does not know what the Canary Islands are. She said it, not Andrew. They had many ideas and plans. They climbed a tree. Andrew drops Joanna off. She runs across her yard with her pizza, jumps over a stump, goes into the house. She could have gone around the stump. It was more fun to leap over the stump, like a gazelle. So that's how you have fun. Andrew sits in his car, feels bored and sarcastic, and starts to drive away. Joanna runs wildly at the car. Andrew is confused. Joanna knocks on Andrew's window; she will invite Andrew inside to 'court' Ashley? Andrew puts the window down. Joanna is grinning. Shit-eating? A normal grin. She pays for the pizza. "Thank you, Andrew," she says, and runs away. Andrew sits in his car thinking about rafting around the Canary Islands with Sara using an inflatable marshmallow raft. A bear comes out of Joanna's house.

Andrew puts the window up.

The bear stares at Andrew.

Andrew puts the window down a little.

"Do you need something?" Andrew says.

"Yeah," the bear says.

"Oh. What do you need?"

"Come here."

The bear points at a house.

"Do you need help?" Andrew says.

"Come here," the bear says.

"Where?"

"Do you want free money?" the bear says.

"Why?"

"Do you want a hundred dollar bill?" the bear says.

"I don't know," Andrew says. He puts the window down all the way. "Why do you have free money?"

"Come here." The bear steps toward the house he pointed at before.

"It's a trick."

"Yes or no," the bear says. "Do you want free money and a free laptop computer or not?"

"I own a home computer."

The bear has a twenty-dollar-bill and a blue blanket and holds them in front and walks to Andrew's car and puts the blanket on Andrew's head and rips off Andrew's door and the top of Andrew's car. The bear picks up Andrew and carries Andrew to the house he earlier pointed at and in the side yard sets down Andrew, who takes the blanket off his own head. The bear kneels, opens a secret passageway under a patch of grass, and points at a ladder that goes underground. Andrew goes to the ladder. "Do it," the bear says.

"Do what?" Andrew says. "Why?"

"Do it," the bear says.

The bear takes the blanket from Andrew and drops it down the passageway.

"Oh," Andrew says. "Good thinking. Good idea. Now I'm required to go get the blanket, or else I'll appear 'irresponsible,' or something,

an irresponsible human being littering in the
wilds of North America. Yeah. I don't know.
Okay."

Andrew climbs down the ladder.

The bear climbs down the ladder.

They climb together.

They are climbing.

The bear kicks Andrew's head.

"Was that your head?" the bear says.

Andrew doesn't say anything.

"Andrew," the bear says. "Was that your
head?"

"Stop talking."

"What was it?" the bear says.

"A laptop computer."

They keep climbing down.

"Where's your sledgehammer?" Andrew
says.

"Sledgehammer," the bear says. "What are
you talking about?"

It gets colder.

The bear makes noises like, "Hrr. Hrr."

"Not all bears are the same bear," the bear
says.

They climb some more and reach a corridor.
Andrew picks up the blanket.
They walk through the corridor.
There is a nook in the corridor.
A moose is lying in the nook.
The moose's eyes are open.
The bear takes the blanket from Andrew.
The bear tells Andrew to keep walking.
"A moose," Andrew says.
"Keep walking," the bear says.
Andrew keeps walking and reaches a cliff.

Below the cliff is a city of dolphins and bears. Sometimes there is a very tall statue of the current president of the United States. Andrew recognizes the president's face.

The bear stands next to Andrew.
"Hrr, hrr," the bear says.
"You're cold," Andrew says.
"It's a cold and lonely world," the bear says.
"Just kidding," the bear says. "Sort of."
"I'm going to sit," Andrew says.

Andrew sits. A dolphin comes from the corridor. Andrew stands. The dolphin has a sledgehammer. Andrew looks at the sledgehammer; the dolphin slaps Andrew's face. More dolphins come from the corridor. The cliff is crowded. More dolphins come; a dolphin is crowded off the cliff; as it falls it goes, "EEEEE EEE EEEE!" Andrew laughs a little. Two more dolphins fall and the cliff is not as crowded anymore. The dolphin with the sledgehammer says, "Watch this." The other dolphins look. The dolphin with the sledgehammer slaps Andrew's face.

"Stupid," says one of the other dolphins.

And throws a smoke bomb.

When the smoke clears there are many bears and no dolphins.

A bears throws a smoke bomb on the floor.

When the smoke clears there is one dolphin. The dolphin slaps Andrew's face, throws a smoke bomb; smoke clears and there is the first bear. Andrew looks at the bear, who is taller than Andrew.

"Are you okay?" the bear says.

Andrew touches his cheek.

It's swollen.

"Are you okay?" the bear says.

"I'm okay," Andrew says. "Are you okay?"

The bear looks at Andrew.

The bear kneels and opens a trapdoor.

There is another ladder.

The bear points at it.

Andrew feels bored.

"No, wait," Andrew says.

"What," the bear says.

"I already did that before."

"There's two more," the bear says.

"I know," Andrew says. "I already went. Uh, the squirrels."

"Hamsters," the bear says.

"I forgot. But I went; do you believe me. The hamsters are sad."

"Go again," the bear says.

"Go again."

"Go again," the bear says. "It'll be fun."

"Do you have a name?" Andrew says. "Do bears have names?"

"Andrew," says the bear.

Andrew feels nervous. "I'm Andrew."

"My name is Andrew," the bear says.

"No," Andrew says.

"Uh, yes," the bear says.

"Oh," Andrew says.

"Go again," the bear says. "We'll have fun."

"How will it be fun?"

"We are both named Andrew," the bear says. "I don't know."

"Your name isn't Andrew," Andrew says.

"My name is Andrew," the bear says. "What the fuck?"

"I don't know," Andrew says. "I'm stupid. I feel stupid."

"Let's go," the bear says.

"How will it be fun?"

The bear scratches the wall and stares at Andrew.

The bear looks at Andrew.

The bear points at the corridor they came from.

Andrew walks there and stands there.

The bear pushes Andrew a little.

Andrew walks through the corridor they came from.

He glances at the nook without moving his neck; there are two aliens standing on a moose.

The moose's head is covered with a blanket.

Andrew keeps walking; the bear is behind him.

He makes it to where the ladder is and stands there.

"The next time I have to point I'll also punch you in your face," the bear says. "And eat you."

"Do it," Andrew says.

The bear makes a fist, slowly moves the fist to Andrew's face, touches Andrew's face with the knuckles, with its other hand holds the back of Andrew's head and slowly smushes Andrew's face into the knuckles of its hand that it had slowly moved toward then touched the front of Andrew's face with; the hand is furry.

"Stop," Andrew says.

The bear stops.

"Do it for real," Andrew says.

The bear punches the air by Andrew's head.

"Do it with good aim," Andrew says. "And with eating. You said 'and eat you.'"

The bear climbs up the ladder.

"Do it with a free laptop computer," Andrew says. "Or I'll kill you."

The bear climbs down and stares at Andrew.

"There's nothing to do," the bear says.

"I know," Andrew says.

The bear looks at Andrew.

"Why were there statues of the president?" Andrew says.

"Life is stupid," the bear says.

"I hate life more than you do."

"No," the bear says.

"Yeah."

"No."

"Yeah."

"No," the bear says and disappears.

Andrew stands there.

Then climbs up the ladder and walks to his car.

The door and the top are back.

Andrew opens the door and the door falls on the street.

He drives out of 'Windy Brook.' The top of the car falls on the street. Why did Joanna become very happy after exiting the car? Don't think about it. Start a band with Steve, if his plane doesn't crash. Romantically pursue Joanna's sister, Ashley, under the pretense of needing a bass player. Don't strategize. Just get her number after fourteen days and start a band under the pretense, somehow, of a killing rampage. E-mail, phone-number, marriage. Martial arts, deer, nothingness. A band can make Andrew happy. Every song will be depressing, which will make Andrew happy. It is not impossible to be happy. One song will be about U-turns. 'Allegorical.' 'Profound.' When Steve comes back from New York City they will start a band. They'll 'screw around' for two hours then feel depressed and go to Denny's. ("Remember when my mom died?") They'll 'jam' for ten minutes and feel bored, and fucked. The word 'jam' embarrasses Andrew a little. 'Screw around.' Andrew needs to go back to Denny's and apologize. He'll throw a wad of cash at the doomed waitress then apologize sincerely. He will not overturn a table. He'll blame Steve. Steve will go to jail. Use fake names. *Thomas ran away, not me. I got caught up in the moment.* Use clichés of language and fake names; give the cash in a manila envelope, smile contritely, apologize sincerely, use one or two clichés of language. *Gotta run, don't spend it all in one place.* It's 9 p.m. Do it tonight? Andrew is better, as a person, at night. In daylight he feels like a bad actor in an independent movie, about to go on a melodramatic killing spree.

At home Andrew writes "Sorry" on an envelope. Below that, "For Real." On another envelope he writes "Really Sorry" and puts two twenties in. Sounds sarcastic. On another, "Sincerely Sorry," moves the twenties. The alliteration is too commercial. Writes "Sorry." Moves the twenties. Andrew feels sorry for the twenties. At least they are a pair. The twenties are in love. Andrew is jealous.

He drives to and parks behind Denny's, turns off the car. *I made a fucking U-turn.* If Sara were here they'd walk around giving away envelopes containing mystery things. One envelope would have three wishes, and it would be real. In the morning they would climb a tree.

There will always be the absence of Sara. There will always be the sad martial arts champion. In the distance there are apartments. There are trees, storage places, a few moose. There is a bear riding a moose like a horse. There is a retirement home with a fence and a moat around it. The fence is not enough. They need the moat in addition to the fence. One manager is not enough. ("Don't rape her.") The sad manager. The sad manager is fucked. Andrew as a small boy slept in the same room as his parents and sometimes woke to them having sex on the carpet. They had sex on the carpet instead of the bed. One time Andrew's mom and dad were fighting in a restaurant. Andrew was seven or eight. His mom was angry that his dad had given her a disease, was how Andrew understood it. Andrew thought it was AIDS. He was crying. He wanted his mom to tell what was wrong because he thought she was going to die. A bear opens Andrew's passenger door and sits in the passenger seat.

"You lied," the bear says.

Andrew does not look at the bear.

"Did you lie?" the bear says.

The bear is breathing loudly.

Andrew stares outside.

There is a tree.

The old people's home.

There will always be the old people's home.

"You lied," the bear says. "You lied and made me sad."

The bear hesitates then leaves.

Andrew's mom said she would tell if Andrew stopped crying. He stopped crying and felt nervous. She said she would tell in the restroom. In the restroom Andrew felt very small. Andrew's mom locked the door. She bent over and said in Andrew's ear that it was herpes— Andrew was looking in the mirror; his eyes were just a little above the counter and he looked at the top part of his head—and that she wouldn't die. Andrew felt very happy and enjoyed his lunch even while his mom and dad kept fighting so that it was uncomfortable for everyone else in the restaurant. After college Andrew kept his job at the library and got another in a movie theatre. They tricked him at the movie theatre and he lost the job. At the library he began to take two-hour lunch breaks; one day they surrounded him and fired him. He had no money left and went home and lived with his parents in Florida. His mom was keeping things from him, he could tell. She had cancer or something but wouldn't talk about it. Andrew's dad was like, *Your mom doesn't want you to know, but I think I should tell you*—and Andrew interrupted and said that if his mom didn't want him to know he shouldn't know. His dad walked away. Whenever there was partial nudity on TV Andrew's dad would say, "This isn't for kids." Even when Andrew was twenty his dad would tell Andrew not to look. He'd say it in a strange tone that was serious and nervous and his face would look meek.

A minivan parks adjacent Andrew. A girl and a boy, and some dolphins, talking loudly and laughing. Andrew leans over and pretends he is looking for something in the passenger seat. He is crying a little. "Your car has no top or driver's side door," says a boy. Andrew stares at the things on the passenger seat. CD

cases, blue pens, a receipt from Albertson's.
He takes the receipt and stares at it, leaned
over in the car. It's dark. He can't see anything. He folds the receipt and puts it in his
pocket. He sits a while then gets out and
walks toward Denny's. He can feel he's about
to start thinking about Sara. He keeps walking and thinks about the future. The future.
He has some vague images of things happening, or not happening, and then it feels like
the future exists, already, for him to go home,
lie in bed, and think about, like a memory; it
feels like the past.

Driving, delivering pizzas. No Sara. No future.
At a stoplight Andrew feels very calm suddenly. Feels like being filmed. He is in Florida,
being filmed for an independent movie starring
someone else. Sara, probably. His life must
change. Things must happen and explode
because of being in a movie. Andrew will teleport into a perilous situation, punch someone
in the face; teleport to Sara, hug her. He was
driving. There was a field and she was like, *We*

should drive into that tree, like a garage. He was like, *Let's climb it and eat in it*. They sat on branches and licked Popsicles.

Light turns green. Andrew doesn't want to go. He goes. He should drive into something. A mountain. The mountain would explode. There's nothing to drive into. If Sara were here there'd be things to drive into, for some reason. Andrew passes the neighborhood he's supposed to turn into and U-turns over the median, knocking over a small tree. A row of cars go by honking. Andrew laughs. He has no future. He is embarrassed for knocking over a tree. That was wrong. Representing Domino's Pizza Corporation. He shouldn't be making illegal U-turns. He feels bad. There were birds in that tree. An enormous family of baby birds, and squirrels. The mother bird will fly back and feel confused.

At home Andrew calls Steve. 10 p.m. Either cards at Justin's or the arcade. Cards will lead to drinking; everyone will end up depressed. Arcade, then. Andrew drives to Steve's house. As Steve is walking to the car his two little sisters throw water balloons. Both miss and land on the grass. The sisters run, pick up the balloons, throw them. One bounces off Steve's face, the other splashes on the driveway. The sisters run to the side yard, do high-fives, and run away.

"I'm going to kill them," Steve says in the car.

"They gave each other high-fives," Andrew says.

"We should go on a killing rampage," Steve says. "In my front yard."

"Good idea." Andrew wishes he were one of the little sisters. He feels depressed suddenly; and bored. He should be one of the sisters and Sara the other. "Now what. Arcade?"

"I hate the arcade," Steve says. "It's depressing and a waste of time. I'm broke."

"I always say things are depressing and a waste of time. Don't steal my identity."

"Go fuck yourself," Steve says.

"I will. Tonight. In my enormous house."

"Yeah," Steve says. "I was giving you a friendly suggestion."

"Yeah." Killing rampage in the arcade. "I should play arcade games and kill myself on purpose and go around saying I'm killing myself."

"Don't kill yourself," Steve says. "Kill my siblings."

"Why do you call them siblings?"

"I'm stupid," Steve says. "Don't kill my siblings. Kill me."

"I killed a tree today. I felt bad. I should kill my job. But with kindness. The kindness of strangers."

"First kill me and my siblings," Steve says.

"I need to use your bathroom."

"Go," Steve says.

Andrew goes into Steve's house. It's very dark inside. Andrew is afraid an alien will grab him. The alien will be lonely and want a hug but Andrew will have a heart attack and a seizure at the same time. Steve's third sister, Ellen, the one in high school, is sitting on the sofa in the living room. She is sitting there, in the dark, not doing anything. She picks up a book and looks at it.

"I'm using the bathroom," Andrew says.

It is very dark in the living room.

Ellen stands and walks away. Her book hits her leg and falls and she walks away faster.

Andrew uses the bathroom then comes out. Ellen is walking very slowly through the living room. She looks a little confused. Andrew follows her to the kitchen. Ellen opens the refrigerator and without bending her back stands looking in.

"What book were you reading?" Andrew says.

"Weren't you reading a book?" Andrew says.

"I don't know," Ellen says. She leaves the refrigerator open and walks away. She comes back and closes the refrigerator. It is very dark without the refrigerator's light. Ellen trips on a chair and falls and stands and walks into another room.

"You took a long time," Steve says in the car.

"I tried to talk to your sister."

"Don't be an asshole," Steve says.

"No, I tried to talk to her for real."

"You are an asshole," Steve says.

"She was sitting in the dark staring. It was good."

"She has no friends," Steve says.

They go to Wal-Mart. They look for something to use against the little sisters. Can't find anything. They stay at Wal-Mart over two hours. In the car Andrew has a videotape, *Gosford Park*.

"You son of a bitch," Steve says.

"Did you see this?"

"You son of a bitch," Steve says again.

Steve on a killing rampage; mass grave in the side yard. "It won every award," Andrew says. "Because the director is a hundred years old or something. It's the Jhumpa Lahiri of movies." Doesn't make sense. Oh well.

"You're the Jhumpa Lahiri of stealing shit from Wal-Mart," Steve says.

"I bought it."

"You bought it with cunning and speed," Steve says.

"Yeah. And a ten dollar bill." Andrew turns on the car. Sara. The music is loud and depressing. Andrew turns it down. "Jhumpa Lahiri makes me want to kill a blue whale or something. I told you about her, right? Yeah. I don't understand her... name. Her name looks like a killing rampage."

"We should hunt her down," Steve says. "With cunning and speed."

"She probably lives on a diamond boat with her Pulitzer Prize." Sara lives in New York City. They had classes together. She drew a penis on Jhumpa Lahiri's face. They went into bookstores. She graduated early, met someone else. Andrew met no one, moved back to Florida, and has no future.

They drive to Justin's house and throw *Gosford Park* in the front yard. Probably five guys inside playing cards and drinking; all depressed, though none will admit it. Five guys drinking, admitting being depressed. They would go on a depressed rampage, killing things languidly. Andrew killed an extended family of birds and squirrels. He climbed a tree with Sara. Her Popsicle was blue. It was strange. It was opaque or something. *Why is your Popsicle confused?*

They drive around, not doing anything; not going anywhere. It's dark and quiet outside. In the car they listen to really depressing music. Andrew feels disorientated and bored, or else lucid and calm; he can't tell. The stereo system is pretty good. Honda Civics are strange. Andrew likes Honda Civics for some reason. They look like how he feels; is that it? Should've leapt to her branch and kissed her. Too dangerous. Should've suggested building a tree fort. *Let's quit school and live in a tree fort. Like a garage.* Wink at her. Sara, laughing. Sometimes she'd laugh maniacally. Sara's beautiful face, laughing insanely. Then calm and pretty.

"What if one of us started crying," Andrew says loudly.

"I'm going to Seattle tomorrow," Steve says. Didn't hear. Music's too loud. Or did he? Doesn't matter. Steve will go to Seattle and never come back. Sara in New York City, Steve in Seattle. Andrew alone in a tree fort, feeling sorry for himself. The mother squirrel staring at an acorn, disillusioned. The little sisters grown up and depressed, sarcastic high-fives in the living room. The balloon, smacking Steve's face. The balloon.

They go to Denny's.

"I need a wife," Steve says in a booth.

"I need...I don't know. I knead bread."

"We'd go on a shopping spree," Steve says. "Then she'd leave me and I'd go on a killing spree."

Sara, married; she's probably married by now. "Remember when the balloon slapped your face?"

"I'm going to kill them," Steve says. "I will never kill anyone."

Sara, laughing marriedly. "Remember..." Sara Tealsden. Stop thinking about Sara. "When I said, 'remember when the balloon slapped your face?'"

"Yeah," Steve says.

"What if your sisters marry each other?"

"We should start a band," Steve says.

Steve in Seattle, drinking coffee with his dad. Steve's dad, screaming. Doesn't make sense.

"We will never start a band," Andrew says. "I want to start a band called 'Lesbian Incest.'" He feels stupid.

"What the fuck is a 'Jhumpa Lahiri?'" Steve says.

"I don't know. I told you about her. Didn't I tell you about her?"

"Yeah," Steve says. "Still. What the fuck is a Jhumpa Lahiri?"

"I don't know. A person."

"It's not a person," Steve says.

The waitress comes, a girl they knew from high school. Andrew doesn't remember her name. They pretend they don't know one another. They order quickly; she leaves. She has gotten fat. Working at Denny's. Her life is over. If Sara worked at Denny's Andrew would smile. Andrew works at Domino's, a more cutting-edge version of Pizza Hut. He should quit. He wants to quit his life like a job. He is writing a book of stories about people who are doomed. He will never commit suicide. He will never kill anyone, start a band, or commit suicide. His girlfriend in college once tried to commit suicide. Then she published a book. Andrew needs to publish a book. Publishing a book will not make him feel less fucked. He cries a little some nights. He worked in a library and a movie theatre in New York City and now works at Domino's, and cries a little some nights. His parents moved to Germany. Germany is a more cutting-edge version of China, maybe.

"I forgot her name," Steve says.

"Starts with an S." No, that's Sara. "Uh, she was in my English class." Mrs. Poole had a bald spot. They put Rogaine brochures on her desk and she pretended it never happened. Sara liked that story. Andrew told her in the tree. He said he wanted to give Mrs. Poole a hug, and three wishes. What else, Sara said. A golden tiara, Andrew said. Sara laughed and said she liked Mrs. Poole. Andrew said he liked Mrs. Poole, then felt depressed and couldn't speak anymore. Sara's Popsicle was depressed.

His was green. "Starts with an F." Should've thrown it at her; danced nimbly in the tree. "I don't know. I just made that up. I have no idea." No future. "I have no future."

"I don't want to think about this shit," Steve says.

"Neither do I. It's depressing." And a waste of time. "What are you doing tomorrow?"

"Seeing my dad," Steve says. "In Seattle."

"Oh yeah. For how long?" Steve's dad, screaming.

"One week or something. I can't wait."

"You really want to see him? When people get enthusiastic I feel like they're being sarcastic. I hate that."

"I sounded enthusiastic?" Steve says.

"Not really. I don't know. You sounded strange."

"I wasn't being sarcastic," Steve says. "I don't really want to see my dad though. Um, I think I meant I can't wait to not have to raise my siblings for one week."

"I can't process what you just said."

"Neither can I," Steve says.

"Good."

"I feel good," Steve says.

"Wait. Aren't your sisters going with you? Who will feed them?"

"Oh yeah," Steve says. "They are coming with me."

Andrew wants to go too. Andrew and Steve, in Seattle, burying Steve's dad in the side yard.

"Wait, no," Steve says. "Ellen is feeding them."

"What if she kills them instead?" Ellen on a depressed rampage, quietly murdering things.

"She's taking summer school to make friends," Steve says. "She has no friends."

"I just thought about going to Seattle with you and murdering your dad. And I keep imagining your dad screaming."

The waitress walks by. She looks depressed and confused. She looks directly at Steve for some reason. She walks by again, confused. She has gained weight and given up on life. She gave up on life then gained a lot of weight. They happened simultaneously, like in a nightmare.

"Why does she hate me?" Steve says. "I'm not going to be able to sleep tonight. Why doesn't she have a nametag? I'm angry. I can't sleep tonight."

"She's trying to subvert the Denny's Corporation. She's against capitalism."

"I'm going to subvert her face with a lead pipe," Steve says.

"I hate faces." Except Sara's. Every face should be Sara's face. That would be scary. If aliens looked like Sara Andrew would hug them and feel calm. Aliens should look like Sara. Andrew should look like Sara. Then Sara would look like Andrew and things would be reversed. The waitress comes back. Steve stares at Andrew. Andrew stares at Steve. Steve has three siblings; 4, 7, and 16, or something. Steve's father left. Andrew wishes Steve were Sara. Why not? The waitress is here with no food or anything. Andrew glances at her face. She looks cutting-edge. Her eyes are a little wet but very clear and pretty. She's not as confused anymore. Her life is not over, after all. Not yet. Soon. She takes the ketchup.

"What a fucking bitch," Steve says, and moves his water to where the salt and pepper are. "I feel like Snoop Dog. Is this what Snoop Dog feels like?" Steve. Andrew likes Steve. He also likes Sara. Sara called people motherfuckers. It made Andrew smile. She did it on purpose sometimes, to make Andrew smile. Andrew would always think about what she did or said and understand that she was very interesting. One time standing in a bookstore she bit Andrew's shoulder and Andrew bled. One time she called the register guy at Duane Reade a motherfucker. *What?* the guy said. *Nothing*, Sara said. The guy's face was blank. He worked at Duane Reade. He was a young black man. A motherfucker. Andrew had to run away to laugh; he ran into an aisle and laughed. Sara pushed him and he fell on a shampoo bottle and it hurt. They came to Florida and climbed a tree. One time in a bookstore she bit Andrew's shoulder and Andrew fell on the floor. Denny's is comparable to Domino's, probably. What is Denny's a more cutting-edge version of? Depressing waste of time. Steve is talking about casinos. He wants to start a Jawbreaker cover band, play in casinos. Mass grave behind a casino. Steve on TV with a lead pipe, *I'm going to kill her.* Reporters, *Who?* Steve, *Jhumpa Lahiri.* Sara, laughing. Snoop Dog, stoned.

"When people are winning money they want to hear sad songs," Steve says. "They want to know even with a lot of money they'll still be alone." He sneezes. "That makes no sense. What if it did, though. Then we'd play Jawbreaker songs in casinos. My plane is going to crash tomorrow."

Andrew realizes he has been staring across Denny's at a man's profile. The man's face is abnormally large. His head is too big and his neck is also very large. Andrew feels very depressed and a little angry. "Look at that guy."

Steve looks. "We should invite him to eat with us, then putt-putt."

"I hope a genie gives him three wishes," Andrew says. Sara, *What else?* "And a lead pipe."

"When I looked we made awkward eye contact. Now I'm enemies with him."

"I can't process what you just said," Andrew says. "Just kidding. I processed it immediately and I think it's funny."

A different waitress brings their food. Her name is Bernadette. They eat for a while. They are eating. ("How do you have fun?") Jawbreaker, *You win, you lose, it's the same old news*. Octopus. Mark was sad about his Octopus. Steve stands. "Andrew," he says. "Come here."

"Wait." Steve in Seattle, playing putt-putt in the rain, with a lead pipe. "What are you doing?"

Bernadette comes back. Steve sits. When Bernadette is gone Steve stands and walks out of the restaurant. Andrew sits very still then stands and leaves without looking at anyone. In the parking lot the waitress without a name and whose life may already be over chases them halfway to their car. Andrew almost runs her over on the way out. Killing rampage. Andrew laughs. Steve has his head outside the window. "Denny's sucks," he screams. His voice cracks.

"She was so depressed," Andrew says. "I wanted to murder her with kindness and love."

"I feel stupid," Steve says. "I felt bad for her too. She was a bitch to us. I don't know. I'm broke. I feel stupid. Did you hear what I yelled?"

"I want to be her. And come kill me. I feel like shit."

"We should go back and apologize sincerely," Steve says. "And then overturn a table."

"And then run away with cunning and speed."

"Yeah," Steve says.

"I'd be overjoyed if someone did that at Domino's. If we had tables." Too cutting-edge for tables. "We don't have tables."

"That was fun," Steve says. "I don't feel stupid."

"I know. I admit it was fun."

"My plane is going to crash," Steve says. "Remember when my mom died?"

"I hate the world," Andrew says. "I'm putting my head out the window to scream 'Fuck.'" He puts down the window, puts his head out, screams "Shit," and puts the window back up.

"The world is stupid," Steve says.

"I feel stupid."

"This is stupid," Steve says. "I don't know what 'this' is."

"I don't know how to have fun."

"My sister is more depressed than both of us," Steve says.

"I feel terrible," Andrew says.

Steve talks some more. While Steve is talking Andrew thinks about conveying that he had an image of Steve playing putt-putt with a lead pipe in the rain, alone, in Seattle, and that the reason Steve was doing that was because he was driving in the rain and listening to music and had felt very happy suddenly, parked the car, and broken into a putt-putt place to play putt-putt alone at around 3 a.m. The sentence is too long. He can't keep it in his head. He feels tired. He feels bored. He wants to scream the word 'shit' at people while driving past them, then maybe follow them home and apologize sincerely before head butting them into a human-colored paste. He drops Steve off. On the way home Arby's, Taco Bell, McDonald's, Walgreen's, Kmart, Starbucks, in a row. Andrew stares at that. He wants to subvert them somehow. He is against capitalism for some reason; something about how it directs human perception away from sentient beings and toward abstractions; he is also against being against things, because the binary nature of the universe is against being against things. Still, he wants to cause destruction to McDonald's. It would be good to subvert all these places. Sara would agree. They'd go in Starbucks, wreak complex and profound havoc. People would scream and make faces of agony and intrigue. At home people would sit with Kleenex and contemplate what had happened, then quietly weep. He and Sara would run to his gigantic house, laughing complexly. The house is enormous. A mansion. No it isn't. Just a large house. A mansion is a large house. Andrew's parents live in a tower in Berlin. Andrew saw photos: eight towers, in a row. In one hundred years the Earth will resemble a metal ball with spikes. It will move shinily through the universe—confused, deadly. Grade-schooler, *Why does the Earth look like a medieval weapon*? When Andrew saw the tower photos he thought of them falling like dominoes. He works at Domino's, a version of Pizza Hut. Something is wrong with his mom. Cancer or something. She won't say what. She is a good person. The man with the enormous head is a good person. Is he? Everything is so good and sad somehow. Andrew is crying a little. It's the music. He is listening to very depressing and catchy music. He should go back to Denny's and throw a wad of cash at a customer's face, and run away. Money won't make that waitress happy. She needs romantic love. She'll never get it. She was confused because of her life being already over. It is impossible to be happy. Michael Fisher sitting in the lobby reading the *New Yorker*. Andrew wants to destroy the world with a series of startling acts of kindness; each successive act more unheard-of than the previous. When Andrew gets home Sara will be there, laughing at the idea of living in a tree fort. They will swim. Why did he think that? Because of having no future.

Next afternoon, eating cereal. Staring at the Lucky Charms box. Andrew is eating Lucky Charms because he has given up on life. He should create Anathema Charms. One time Andrew's mom came home with Lucky Charms instead of Cheerios. She was happy and held the Lucky Charms in her right hand, not in a grocery bag. When Andrew saw the Lucky Charms it made him happy. They were in the kitchen and were both very happy about the unhealthy change from Cheerios to Lucky Charms. Now Andrew just feels like Snoop Dog all the time. No he doesn't. He hasn't once felt like Snoop Dog. "That was Steve," Andrew says out loud, for some reason. He feels nauseous. He'll never see Sara again. What if Jhumpa Lahiri were in love with him? Would he spurn her? She lives on a diamond-studded cruise ship. Her Pulitzer Prize is afraid of her. Andrew grins. As a person, he is lonelier than Sara. She is shorter. Sara Tealsden. Thinking her last name makes Andrew feel miserable and good. Sara Tealsden. Andrew will cry. He should throw the Lucky Charms. Marshmallows, flying through the air. He does it. The box hits the refrigerator and falls to the ground. No marshmallows. No future.

He feeds his dogs, takes them out, brings them in; makes coffee, showers, drinks coffee.

He passes the piano room on the way to the computer room. There is fresh dog shit in the middle of the piano room. Clean it later. There's also dog piss. Son of a bitch. Steve in

Seattle, high-fiving his dad. *Go back and apologize. And then overturn a table.* Steve.

In the computer room Andrew stares at the table of contents of his story collection. His story-collection. Rejected by over thirty editors. Rejection is good. Putting others ahead of self, giving things away. Success, money, power, fame, happiness, friends; any kind of pleasure— giving it all away, in the pyramid scheme of life, with the knowledge that everything will be returned, and being satisfied with that knowledge; not with the actual return of things, but the idea of the return of things. There is no return of things. There is death. Martial arts, deer, death. Singapore, octopus, death. In each story the main character is depressed and lonely. Every story is twenty-pages and about pointlessness. He opens one of the stories. If he writes good and funny enough, Sara will materialize in the swimming pool. He stares at the story. Delete it. He needs coffee. He already had coffee. Move the story casually to the recycling bin. Empty the recycling bin with cunning and speed. Start a band. *You win, you lose. It's the same old news.* Write a story about Steve. Killing rampage in a casino, with lead pipes. Compare and contrast Jhumpa Lahiri and Snoop Dog. It would be funny to kill someone with the Pulitzer Prize. Focus. Andrew has worked for maybe two hundred hours on this story. How did this happen? The story is incomprehensible; rejected over twenty times. He has e-mailed it to people. No one says anything. There is no communication. Stevie Smith, *I was much farther out than you thought.* Stevie's oeuvre, sitting there someplace, confused. Music is better. You can't lie in bed with an audio book and cry and feel miserable and good. Maybe you can. Jhumpa Lahiri will never go on a depressed killing rampage. Snoop Dog, maybe. Jhumpa Lahiri. The *New Yorker.* One of her stories is called "Sexy." Sexy. Sara is sexy. Sara, laughing sexily.

Andrew stands.

He lies on the carpet.

He stares at the carpet. Mark.

Mark likes Spiderman more.

Andrew drives to work. Music's too loud. He turns it off. His parents live in a tower; one of eight. Which one? The cancer one. Sara is in the passenger seat. Andrew looks. She isn't there. If she were she would point at something and they would climb it. A mountain. There would be mountains. Andrew would hug her. He doesn't want to deliver pizzas. He wants to build a tree fort. Everyone at work will be trite and clichéd. Andrew is trite and clichéd. He has nothing to say to anyone. No one has anything to say to anyone, for some reason. Everything is clichéd and melodramatic. Andrew's girlfriend in college tried to kill herself once with Valium from a tooth operation. It made Andrew feel clichéd and melodramatic. He should have laughed maniacally at her, then killed her with a lead pipe. Him and Sara, laughing sexily at the ex's corpse. Kiss her while she's laughing sexily. While they're still in the tree. Marry her with cunning and speed, then kill her, for some reason. Andrew should sell his gigantic house and move to New York City. He would carry his cash in a suitcase. Sara would be there, laughing. They would stand in bookstores. They would hunt down Jhumpa Lahiri and follow her sheepishly with lead pipes. *Let's build a tree fort on her face.* Sara would call one of those cops on horses a motherfucker. The cop would avert his eyes. Sara would ask directions for the wild wild west.

At a stoplight everything is calm and quiet. Andrew has the feeling of being filmed. Happens every time at this stoplight. Things must explode. Andrew's life must change in a trite, clichéd, and melodramatic way. He puts his head out his window and halfheartedly screams. If Sara were here she'd laugh. The light turns green. If Andrew drives ridiculously fast, and insanely, Sara will sense it in New York City, or wherever she is. Andrew drives very fast and sideswipes across two lanes while making an insane turn through an intersection. At work he delivers four pizzas and then delivers Buffalo wings to an old man in pajamas. It is seven p.m. Andrew goes back to his car. There is a dolphin in the backseat.

Andrew drives back to Domino's.

"Matt," he says. "There's a dolphin in the backseat. Can I go home?"

"Let me put these pepperonis on," Matt says. "Then I'll cash you out."

After being paid sixty-cents gas money for each delivery Andrew has fourteen dollars.

"Give half to the dolphin," Matt says.

They are in Matt's office.

"Okay," Andrew says. "Wait. Why?"

"Don't ask questions," Matt says. "I'm tired of your insubordination."

"Okay."

"Okay," Matt says. "Open the door but don't leave this office."

Andrew opens the door.

"Jeremy," Matt shouts.

Jeremy comes in the office.

The office is small.

It is a little crowded with three people.

"Yeah?" Jeremy says.

"Get everyone to come in here," Matt says.

Jeremy leaves.

Andrew leaves.

"Andrew," Matt shouts.

Andrew comes back.

"The dolphin can wait," Matt says.

Jeremy comes back with everyone.

They all go into Matt's office.

There is not enough space.

Some people stand on Matt's desk.

Someone closes the door.

It's very crowded.

Someone turns off the light.

The only window is blocked by someone's body.

Andrew can't see anything or move.

It's very hot and dark.

"Whoever just elbowed my face," Matt says. "You're fired."

"Whoever did it," someone says in an affected voice, "just don't say anything."

"But move away from Matt," says a different voice. "When the lights go on. So he won't see. If we ever leave, I mean."

"This is Matt and I's office," Jeremy says. "Everyone calls it 'Matt's office.' It's both of ours."

TAO LIN

"The sad manager," Andrew says.

"Andrew?" Jeremy says.

"I'm scared," someone says.

"I'm bored," Andrew says. "I'm sweating."

"Is Rachel here?" someone else says.

"No," someone says.

Half a minute passes.

"What were you going to say about me?" Rachel says.

"I don't know," someone says.

"I'm confused," someone says.

"Someone open the door," Matt says.

Someone opens the door.

"Now what," someone says.

"I don't know," someone else says.

"Andrew," Jeremy says.

"Everyone should go back to work," Matt says.

"Are you sure?" someone says. "Maybe we should go back to something else. I don't know—just something else."

But everyone has already gone back to work.

Andrew is at his car.

He gives the dolphin seven dollars.

The dolphin goes, "EEEEE EEE EEEE."

Andrew drives toward his house.

At the first stoplight the dolphin says, "Drop me off at Kmart."

"What Kmart? Where's a Kmart?"

"By the diamond store," the dolphin says.

"That's Target."

"Drop me off at Target," the dolphin says.

"That's far."

"So?" the dolphin says.

"Are you buying drugs?"

"Why did you ask me if I'm buying drugs?" the dolphin says. "You're being stupid."

Andrew drives to Target, parks, gets out of the car.

"You don't have to walk me in," the dolphin says.

"I need toilet paper," Andrew says.

The dolphin walks faster than Andrew, then slows a little.

Andrew walks in a different direction a little.

The dolphin sees and walks in an angle away from Andrew.

TAO LIN

When they get to the entrance they get there together.

"Don't be stupid and awkward," the dolphin says. "You want to walk together or not?"

"Fine," Andrew says. "Wait. Are you going to…"

The dolphin stares at Andrew. "Forget it," the dolphin says.

"No, wait," Andrew says. "What are you buying?"

"Get away from me," the dolphin says. "You were going to say if I was going to go 'Eeeee eee eeee.' You are a stupid piece of shit. Go away from me." The dolphin looks at Andrew.

"Wait," Andrew says.

The dolphin goes into the center of a circular clothing rack and quietly cries.

Andrew looks around.

He goes home.

The dolphin cries a while then buys a steak knife.

The dolphin goes home.

It looks in the mirror.

It puts the tip of the steak knife perpendicular to its neck and grips the handle hard.

It stares in the mirror.

It puts on a jacket, takes a plane to Hollywood, and finds Elijah Wood.

"Come somewhere with me," the dolphin says.

"Can I get a river ride?" Elijah says.

"Hold onto my flippers."

Elijah climbs the dolphin's back.

"You are fucking stupid. Hold on when we get to the river," the dolphin says. "Not in the fucking parking lot."

Elijah laughs.

"You are an idiot," the dolphin says.

They take Elijah's car to the ocean.

On the beach the dolphin lies in the water.

Elijah climbs on the dolphin.

The dolphin swims.

"Yeah!" Elijah says.

The dolphin swims to an island.

"I need to get something," the dolphin says.

The dolphin leaves and returns with a heavy branch behind its back.

"You know *The Ice Storm*?" Elijah Wood says. "At the end of the book the guy sees a superhero or something. That was strange. They didn't have it in the movie. Christina Ricci was in the movie."

The dolphin clubs Elijah Wood's head.

Elijah Wood runs away and falls.

The dolphin clubs Elijah's body and legs.

Elijah screams.

The dolphin drags Elijah's corpse into a cave and sits on it.

The cave is very quiet and dark.

The dolphin feels bad.

It feels very calm and a little bad.

A bear drags in Sean Penn's corpse.

The dolphin pushes Elijah's corpse into a hole and there is a loud coconut sound.

The bear pauses then quickly drags Sean Penn's corpse out of the cave.

Sean Penn's skull makes little coconut sounds against the cave floor.

At home Andrew showers and eats a banana. He takes his dogs for a walk. The dogs are tiny. Living with two dogs in an enormous house in a gated community. Andrew's neighbors think he is strange. 'Eccentric.' Andrew is afraid of his neighbors. The gate has a secret pass code. Sara has a secret pass code. She should. Andrew would stand there for years trying combinations. He wouldn't keep track or develop a strategy but just continue trying different combinations and then Kafka would rise from the grave and write a novel about him. He feeds his dogs. There is more dog shit in the piano room. Leave it. Sell the house. Suitcase full of cash. He goes to the back porch. He thinks about jumping into the pool, swimming twenty laps at lightning-speed. Drowning. Putt-putt, he thinks. He goes in the living room. He lies on the sofa. Not waving but drowning. No future. The future is now. Meaningless. Wave of the future. Everything is clichéd and melodramatic. He should eat. He used to think things like, *This organic soymilk will make me healthy and that'll make my brain work better and that'll improve my writing.* Also things like, *The less I eat and the less money I spend on publicly owned companies the less pain and suffering will exist in the world.* Now he thinks things like, *It is impossible to be happy.* Why would anyone think that? Things like, *Godsford Park is the worst movie ever.* Gosford? Godsford?

"Godsford," Andrew says out loud. "Gosford."

"What is happening right now is a depressing waste of time," he says.

He finds his dogs and follows them. "Dogs," he says. Chihuahuas. They have names. Waste of time? No, the dogs are good. They're old. Andrew feels sorry for them. Pretend they are Sara. "Sara," he says. He touches the dogs. They run away. His house is enormous. He'll never find his dogs. He'll find them and crush them. Mass grave. The Earth is just a massive grave. Andrew needs to stop thinking about the things he always thinks about. He needs to sell his house. He needs to clean the dog shit in the piano room. He goes to the piano room with toilet paper. Play a song for Sara. She will sense it. He badly plays fantasie-impromptu. Sounds clichéd and melodramatic. Too loud. Turn it off. He stops playing. Thank you, he thinks. Clean the dog shit later. Never clean the dog shit. Sell the house. *Don't look there, it's just a piano. Don't step there. Don't step on my abstract art.* Sara, *The tree in the front yard doubles as a garage.* Suitcase full of cash. High-fives in the side yard. Ellen, sitting in darkness in the living room. Sara Tealsden. Why is Andrew obsessed with Sara today? Is it like this every day? He can't remember. Don't think about it. Death. Think about death. The binary nature of the universe. Andrew's mom in Germany, staring at a ceiling thinking about death. The mother squirrel flying by, confused. Sara, *I feel like flying squirrels need to stop screwing around and get day jobs.* You win, you lose. The man with the face. Three wishes. Sara. Andrew will scream, sexily. Killing rampage in a tree fort. Andrew is about to murder someone. He goes upstairs into his room, puts on a depressing CD, lies on the floor on his back; pulls his blanket off his bed, covers himself on the floor. Sara.

There is a very loud noise downstairs.

Something is coming up the stairs.

Andrew stands and walks to his bed.

Sits on it.

A bear walks into Andrew's room.

The bear stares at Andrew.

While staring at Andrew the bear claws the wall.

The bear sees the thermostat and turns it

down.

Andrew lies on his bed and falls asleep.

When he wakes it's colder.

The bear is standing going, "Hrr, hrr."

"Polar bear," Andrew says. "Is that what you want?"

The bear stares at Andrew.

Still staring at Andrew goes to Andrew's desk and picks up a CD case.

Looks at the CD case, looks at Andrew, puts the CD case back.

"Put it back," Andrew says. "Oh, okay."

"I just put it back," the bear says.

"I know."

"I need to get something," the bear says.

The bear goes downstairs and comes back with a sledgehammer.

The bear smashes a hole in the floor with the sledgehammer.

The bear looks at Andrew.

The bear feigns jumping into the hole

The bear hops and disappears in the air.

Andrew goes to his window.

The bear is running across the neighbor's

front yard.

The bear jumps over a row of bushes and falls on the grass.

Smashes the bushes with the sledgehammer.

Changes into a truck and drives over the bushes.

Changes back into a bear.

Smashes a tree with the sledgehammer and screams.

Disappears.

Reappears next to Andrew and hugs Andrew.

"I'm sad," the bear says. "Give me advice."

"I don't know. Go to Japan," Andrew says. "It's morning in Japan."

"Where in Japan?"

"A house," Andrew says.

"A house. What city?"

"A house by a river," Andrew says

"Okay," the bear says, and disappears.

Andrew goes to his bed.

He covers himself with the blanket.

Puts his face in the pillow.

Spring break. She came to Florida. She

drew genitals on Jhumpa Lahiri's face. Duane Reade. She was like, *Nothing*. The guy was like, *What?* They sat on separate branches. He should have moved closer. He was too depressed. He is always too depressed. Should've been happier and laughing. He forgot to be happy. He was too bored to be happy. *Your Popsicle looks disorientated*. Sara, laughing. Should have hopped nimbly to her branch, kissed her. Should have held her suddenly and danced. They should've stayed in Florida. They should have danced and fell from the tree and they both should have been taken to a hospital. Together in a hospital kissing. Why isn't that happening right now?

"Batman's car looks like a tank," Andrew said to Mark, in a Japanese restaurant, in Manhattan, where neither of them lived. "Is he making fun of himself? It's like he's just screwing around."

"Maybe I shouldn't see this with you," Mark said. They were going to see the new Batman movie. Mark liked Batman very much but liked Spiderman more. "I'll see it alone."

"I want to see it," Andrew said. "I think if I really wanted I could enjoy it sincerely. I mean, I could 'get lost in the story,' or whatever. If I chose to. Should I?"

"It's not 'getting lost in the story,'" Mark said. "It's just—it's *Batman*. You are a snob."

"No I'm not. I liked *Braveheart*, starring Mel Gibson." Andrew grinned. Shit-eating grin, he thought. Mark did not respond. He was a graduate student, Andrew knew, from Singapore, where in the army one night they screened *Braveheart* in an auditorium, then lectured on patriotism, citing scenes from *Braveheart*. "Is this The Beatles?" Andrew said. They were playing The Beatles, or something, in the Japanese restaurant. "It sounds like it might be The Beatles."

"It is. I like The Beatles."

Andrew looked around without processing anything except that he was currently 'looking around.' He drank his water—all of it—then set it down and looked at it. Singapore, he knew, was its own capital. Like Vatican City. Only Catholics lived in Vatican City. To get in you had to get the Pope to stamp your pass-port. He stamped one hour each day, except Sunday, walking around or sitting on a bench somewhere. You had to find him. Sometimes he climbed a tree to hide. Sara, Andrew thought. None of this was true, he thought, and felt momentarily enlightened—detached from meaning, language, and understanding. "The Beatles…" he said. "Are they—do they believe in God?"

"I don't know," Mark said. "I wouldn't put it above them. Or below them. Whatever."

"They have one song where he's like, 'Jesus loves you,' or something."

"No," Mark said. "That's someone else."

"Oh," Andrew said. "Who?"

"I don't know," Mark said.

Andrew picked up the hot pepper. He felt tired. He existentially had the urge to repeated-ly say, 'I'm bored,' even if he was not bored. He was always bored. Whenever he said some-thing not 'I'm bored' he felt a little agitated, and censored.

"American rock music," Mark said.

They ate without talking. A few weeks ago it seemed like they might become good friends. At night walking near Union Square Mark had said, "Can I ask you a question?" Andrew expected a question about himself. "How do you have fun?" Mark said. "I never had fun, growing up. I don't know how." Andrew wanted to hug Mark, or something—give him three wishes—but instead said that Jean Rhys also said she never had fun growing up. "Read *Good Morning, Midnight*, by Jean Rhys," Andrew said. Another time Mark told Andrew a story (In a café one Friday night, Mark overheard a person talking to the waitress about boredom. The person left. Mark went to the waitress and said, "I'm bored too." The waitress said, "Boring people are bored." Mark paid for his tea and left.). And Andrew told Mark a story (After writing class one time the teacher congratulated Andrew on winning the undergraduate writing prize. "What did you win it for?" said a classmate, Sara. "A story," Andrew said. "What story?" "Something you haven't read," Andrew said. "Why haven't I read it?" "Because I have about ten stories you haven't read." "Can I read them?" "All of them?" "Yeah." "You won't read them. Stop being polite. You are out of control." "I'm not being polite." "I'll e-mail one of them," Andrew said. "Okay," Sara said, and never read it, then graduated and moved home to Massachusetts, from where she said three or four times, on instant messenger, that she would visit Andrew, and, almost a year later, now, hasn't.).

"What do you think about the president?" Andrew said.

Mark put noodles into his mouth.

"I think he's smarter than people think," Andrew said. "He winked on TV. He winked fast, so only a few people would see. I feel like he's being ironic all the time." Andrew stopped talking. Mark did not respond. "I mean everyone on TV is being ironic all the time," Andrew said. "But the president knows he's being ironic all the time, so he's twice ironic. You have to be twice ironic on TV to be regular ironic in real life. So if you're not ironic on TV you're negative ironic in real life. That sounds good. Negative Ironic." Sounded like a rap-metal band with a right-wing fan base, or else an inchoately independent but then MTV-funded movie with a nihilistic premise but a feel-good ending, that came out last year—that always came out last year.

"Irony is so privileged," Mark said. "It's what happens when you don't need to do anything to survive—it's when the things you do have nothing to do with survival and you spend forty million dollars to make Steve Zissou and the Atomic Submarine or whatever it's called."

"I know," Andrew said. "What do you want people to do then?"

"I don't know," Mark said. "Stop being so—you know, I mean, people now, they're all like, 'I'm depressed. You're depressed. Let's get together and be depressed.'"

"That's a good name for a movie," Andrew said. "I'd watch that movie. You would too. Admit it."

"I don't think I would. I'm not like you. You think I am."

"You're from Singapore."

Andrew watched the new Batman movie without irony, sincerity, or enjoyment; or maybe a little enjoyment. Outside, he began then did not stop making jokes about believ-ability, pacing, Batman's smoothies, and Hollywood. Mark said all Andrew did was go around complaining all the time, which was pointless. Andrew apologized, then said he was just being himself—and wasn't even complain-ing, really, just making jokes. Mark transposed his interpretation of Andrew's personality onto modern society and complained about that for a while, citing postmodernism, white people, and Miranda July. Andrew stopped paying attention at white people and thought vaguely about Sara. ("Why haven't I read it?") Mark talked about how he should've seen the movie by himself. Andrew told Mark to stop saying that. Mark said it again, using different words. Andrew said he should be able to move faster and hurt things. He felt very slow and handi-capped, because of Batman, who was absurd and an ironic joke—not to be appreciated without a lot of sarcasm, even by ten-year-olds. He said Mark was right; all he did was complain all the time. A long time ago Andrew's friend Steve in Florida said *All I can do is complain, why?* and Andrew liked it; then one time Sara said *All I do is complain* and Andrew liked that; now Andrew was saying "All I can do is complain, why?" and no one liked it.

"You ruined *Batman* for me," Mark said. "I hate you."

"No you don't," Andrew said. "Stop saying that." He asked Mark about liking Spiderman more than Batman. Mark explained. Andrew understood after the first sentence and stopped listening as Mark gave supporting evidence. They were on Third Avenue in New York City, walking around a bit aimlessly. ("How do you have fun?") People were laughing because of being in Manhattan, drunk, on a Friday night—was that why? Tomorrow it would be Saturday. At work in the library Andrew would check his e-mail. At night he would work on a short story, the theme of which was that the

TAO LIN

main character was doomed, logically, since everyone was doomed. Every sentence would have to say something about that theme or else Andrew would feel that both the story and himself were 'fucked.' It was tedious and mostly unrewarding work (trying to be impersonal and interesting about the more despairing parts of one's past or imagined future) but sometimes, if he wrote lucidly enough, Andrew would feel, in a way that momentarily made him believe despair was a mistake, that he missed those times, that there was a yearning, really, to his prose; and would try, then, to desire, in this missed and wanting and therefore nostalgic way, the present moment, when feeling lonely or sad; to experience it while it was happening as the thing he would later yearn for—to realize, as it was happening, that feeling bad was a mistake—as if it were words on a page, being read not lived. Schopenhauer had said that—that life was to be perceived not as a book you would write but as a book already written, something to be gotten through, so as to detach oneself from suffering, which was an outside thing, really; not actually in the text. Everything was to be accepted. The world was here. Everything was here. Mark liked Spiderman more. As it existed in what was here, in the world, that 'Mark liked Spiderman more,' Andrew knew, it similarly existed that 'Andrew.' He was sort of trying to explain this to Mark but then stopped and said, "I feel confused."

"I don't know why you're so depressed," Mark said. "You have friends. I have no friends."

"I don't have friends. I'm not depressed anyway."

"If you weren't depressed you'd enjoy *Batman* instead of complaining about it," Mark said.

"I did enjoy it," Andrew said. "And I complain when I'm happy."

They walked one block without talking.

"I wish Batman was depressed," Andrew said. "He would lay in bed in his Batsuit all day. We should make that movie."

"We should," Mark said. "Alfred would bring anti-depressant smoothies each morning."

"Robin would watch TV and get drunk," Andrew said. "His dialogue would be, 'I'm a day-time drunk.' And they'd show Batman hiding in a cave. It would do a close-up of Batman's face and he'd be shivering between his eyes, with intensity."

"You'd like that. You'd like it if everyone in the world was depressed," Mark said. "That's the only reason you like me probably," he said hesitantly.

"No," Andrew said.

They stared at a red light, and waited, then crossed the street.

"I don't like happy people," Andrew said. "They're already happy; they don't need to be liked."

"Wow, so selfless," Mark said. "You're a saint. I commend your selflessness. Amazing."

"Sometimes you get sarcastic like that," Andrew said. "It's good. How can you be that sarcastic and still sincerely enjoy *Batman*?"

"Because I'm not a snob."

"Oh."

There was a dark alleyway and Andrew saw an alien, behind which was a moose.

A bear pushed Mark and Andrew into the dark alleyway.

"Watch," the bear said.

The bear disappeared and appeared three feet to the left.

"What did I just do?" the bear said.

"Teleport," Mark said.

The bear disappeared and appeared one foot above the ground and dropped to the ground and bent at the knees a little.

The bear disappeared and appeared laying on its back.

The bear disappeared and appeared standing five feet away.

"I'm bored," the bear said. "I'm teleporting."

The bear walked to Mark.

The bear shoved Mark's shoulder a little.

"I'm bored," the bear said.

Mark took out a twenty-dollar-bill and held it at the bear.

The bear stared at Andrew.

"I'm bored too," Andrew said.

The bear disappeared.

Something bumped into Andrew from behind.

Andrew turned around.

The alien.

Andrew ran away.

He walked in a deli and bought carrot juice.

Mark walked up to Andrew.

"Hey," Mark said, and looked at Andrew's face, then quickly to the side of Andrew's face; lately he always looked to the side a little. "Are you hungry?"

"Do you want to eat?" Andrew said.

"I don't know. I could eat."

"Let's eat, I guess."

They went to a Japanese restaurant, a different one. The Japanese had invented female robots, that year, that danced with you, Andrew somehow knew. He had been to Japan before—once. He should be there now. He would walk on Third Avenue in Japan. There would be a Third Avenue there too. Robots would serenade him. "Japan is better than New

York City," he said. He didn't want to elaborate. It would take forever to elaborate. Someone would eventually realize that the conversation was just a matter of semantics. Was there even a point to talking? "Never mind," Andrew said. "I don't know." Not wanting to elaborate, that was the symptom of something—something bad. Andrew didn't want to think about it. Maybe he should take anti-depressant medicine. ("Alfred would bring him anti-depressants....") See a doctor, fill out forms, wait three weeks for it to 'kick in'—too hard, of course. Why three weeks? Didn't seem right. Should be gradual. Semantics, probably. 'Kick in.' Mark wasn't talking anymore. It was March. March, Andrew thought. He sometimes felt that life was something that had already risen, and all this, the Jackson Pollack of spring, summer, and fall, the vague refrigeration and tinfoiled sky of wintertime, was just a falling, really, originward, in a kind of correction, as if by spiritual gravity, towards the wiser consciousness—or consciousnessless, maybe; could gravity trick itself like that?—of death. It was a kind of movement both very slow and very fast; there was both too much and not enough time to think. They were staring at their menus. They weren't talking to one another anymore. They were acquaintances. They wouldn't hang out anymore after tonight, Andrew knew. He would never see Mark again. Also, Mark would never speak again. The waitress came. They ordered but kept their menus—to stare at.

"They gave me all the bad fish," Mark said later about his seafood salad.

"No, you have all kinds," Andrew said. "What do you like then?"

"Tuna, salmon."

"You have tuna and salmon." He did; they were both there.

"I have—what's this? Squid."

"Octopus," Andrew said.

"Octopus."

"It's octopus," Andrew said.

"Octopus," Mark said.

A hamster was on the wall in the bear's kitchen when the bear appeared.

The bear appeared sitting in a chair.

The hamster ran like a spider across the wall, the ceiling, and another wall.

The bear went to his bedroom.

"My heart is fast," the bear said to his girlfriend.

"Your heart?" the bear's girlfriend said. "Why?"

"A hamster," the bear said.

"Come here," the bear's girlfriend said.

"I don't feel like sex," the bear said.

The bear's girlfriend took the blanket into the kitchen.

The hamster was sitting on the table.

It leapt to the wall and ran across the wall.

The bear's girlfriend went into the bedroom.

The bear was on the bed.

The bear's girlfriend lay on the bed.

"I don't want to exert effort," the bear said. "I don't want to move or think anymore."

"Blow-job," the bear's girlfriend said. "Don't be passive-aggressive."

"I don't want one. I'm just saying how I feel."

The bear's girlfriend rolled off the bed then ran into the kitchen. The hamster was sitting on the table.

And the bear's girlfriend put the blanket on the hamster.

The bear came into the kitchen.

"It will suffocate," the bear said.

The hamster chewed through the blanket.

The hamster stood there.

"I didn't know they do that," the bear's girlfriend said.

"I saw it before," the bear said.

"You just said it would die," the bear's girlfriend said. "You said 'suffocate.'"

"I forgot," the bear said.

"I was talking about myself," the bear said. "It feels like I'm suffocating."

"Your conversation is interminable," the hamster said.

"I know," the bear said.

The bear's girlfriend sat at the table and held the hamster.

The bear's girlfriend slapped the hamster softly in the hamster's face.

The bear sat at the table.

"I want to kill Saul Bellow," the bear said. "I know he is already dead."

"Do you still hate your novel?" the bear's girlfriend said.

"My novel is stupid," the bear said.

"I want to chew through something," the bear's girlfriend said.

"I feel like I'm upside down right now," the bear said. "It feels bad. I feel terrible."

The hamster was asleep.

"It fell asleep from our conversation," the bear's girlfriend said.

"I should take Viagra, anti-depressant medicine, Ritalin, and Caffeine tablets at the same time," the bear said. "Then vomit in a bucket. And take a bath in the swimming pool."

"It's pretending," the bear's girlfriend said. "To avoid having to talk to us."

"It's making fun of us," the bear said. "How boring we are."

"I think I just fell asleep," the bear's girlfriend said. "That's how boring this is right now."

"I want to slap a moose," the bear said.

Sometimes moose would be sleeping and they would feel something. They woke and were being slapped by a bear. But they were not angry. Moose had no delusions that year. They knew there were facts and that the world itself was a fact and that facts were not good or bad but just there—a worldview that happened sometimes after you suffered for a long time, alone, in your room, physically comfortable and listening to music—and so had no opinions, feelings, fear, or hatred. They saw the bears with the blankets and they said, "Thank you."

Sometimes a bear would feel cold.

And go, "Hrr, hrr."

And take a blanket from a moose's head and slap the moose's face.

The moose would say, "Thank you."

Moose that year stood alone in shadowy alleyways. They weighed a thousand pounds, which made them not want to have thoughts. Mostly they just watched, from a distance—in blackness and without thinking. If some of the alleyway was bright and some was dark the moose would walk to where it was dark and stare at where it was bright—and not think anything at all. Sometimes an alien would stand with a moose, not because of solidarity but because of accidentally doing it. Aliens usually stood in dark doorways but sometimes got confused and stood in alleyways behind, on top of, or adjacent moose. Sometimes a bear climbed a moose and the moose would feel warm and happy, which made them run. Moose had no friends that year. A lot of the time a moose would feel tired and lean against other moose. Only there wouldn't be moose there and the moose would fall.

It was sad to see a moose on the ground with its eyeballs round and looking.

So a bear would sometimes put a blanket over a moose's face.

Bears liked to put blankets on things.

Sometimes a bear accidentally wished to have Sean Penn there.

The bear would be watching TV.

Thinking about the Pulitzer Prize.

And go blank a little.

And think, "I wish I could punch Sean Penn in Sean Penn's face."

And Sean Penn would be there.

Sean Penn would fight the bear when it got there.

The bear would try to stop Sean Penn but Sean Penn had knives and the bear would crush Sean Penn by accident.

The bear would think, "Oh god, oh my god."

Then put a blanket on Sean Penn's corpse's head.

It was a year, that year, Ellen knew, as she'd noticed from her 10th grade classmates and from observing her family—her new year's resolution (it was stupid to have one but she was bored in class and made a list, then picked one) had been to be more alert, to think more truthfully about things, and it had affected her, she guessed, with better grades, an increase in self-esteem that was actually just a realization of how dumb everyone was, and nerdy, slightly annoying insights like this one—for doing something not even that exciting or wild and then saying, "Why not?" Or else saying, "Why not?" then doing something sort of forced and meaningless. Mostly people just went around saying, "Why not?" and, later on, when it came time to act, saying, "It's too hard," without ever actually doing anything.

Things still happened that year, of course, like any other year—they were pretty much all the same, Ellen guessed; what was a year, anyway; floating around the sun in the straight line, really, of a circle; it felt sarcastic to keep count—just mostly by accident, or else by momentum, by implication and solution of past things (like a math equation, trying to solve itself, as what was the world, the unstoppable mass of it, but one of those long division problems in seventh grade that went on, annoying and blameless, forever?).

Ellen herself had knocked down a No U-Turn sign. She was sixteen and didn't have a permit and didn't want one—driving was bad

for the environment, she had no money for a
car, and she didn't want to stand in line five
hours to fail whatever stupid test—but had
craved alfalfa sprouts with balsamic vinaigrette
one night when everyone else was asleep, and
so had washed her face and ran out to the
street, to her brother Steve's Honda Civic, the
keys of which were left on the dash (more
depressively, Ellen thought in a tic of imposi-
tion, than stupidly). After knocking down the
No U-Turn sign she panicked and drove for a
time on the wrong side of the road, where,
after a vision of crash test dummies, she felt a
vacuum-sealed sort of calmness—the sound-
reducing serenity of breaking a traffic law, of
going metaphysically back in time, to a truer
place, where every direction was equally legal;
probably this was not unlike meditation, Ellen
thought gently—then cut across a median,
knocking the right rearview mirror against a
tree so that it banged shut against the window,
and drove back to her neighborhood. At her
house, thinking, *Destroy the evidence*, she
parked, put the keys back on the dash, and

then was wrenching the damaged rearview mirror off the car, though not without a lot of difficulty—and not without realizing, after a moment, that there wasn't actually anything wrong with it, it just needed to be adjusted back into position; but continuing, still, with two hands, now, in a sort of rampage—and then was running across the street and lobbing the half-melon of the thing over a fence, into someone's backyard. Back in her house, she walked around carefully, civil and perceiving as a saint. She saw her brother, Steve, asleep on the sofa. In the kitchen her two little sisters were eating a bowl of something, which they hid as Ellen walked by, into her room, where she crawled onto her bed and lay on her side, and, for a long time, then, until she yawned and closed her eyes and fell asleep, stared, a bit objectively, without mood or judgment—though self-consciously so, feeling while doing it a bit empty and melodramatic—at the other side of her room, where the bookcase, the computer, the desk, and the stereo were.

That was in the wintertime, and then it was Spring, and some nights, now, in bed, feeling very bored and a little lonely, Ellen would let herself worry that she had hit a person—that the person had looked like a No U-Turn sign; was wearing a cowboy hat, or something—and then have imaginary conversations with kids at school she wished she were friends with, the ones who listened to punk music like she did and who always dressed prettily and had very beautiful and vividly dyed hair.

"I think I hit a person."

"No you didn't."

"I knocked down a No U-Turn sign. That's illegal."

"You're being honest right now. You can use that to cancel out the sign."

"I'll tell the judge, 'We're even now.'"

"The judge will be like, 'Fine then. Uh, I mean case dismissed.'"

Alert and awake, under her blanket, having these conversations, she would sometimes feel so yearning and friendless and unhelpable—

each moment of being herself, she knew, was a strengthening, an adapting, of who she was; and she didn't want to be who she was—that she would squeak a little.

In Ellen's English class someone said, "I hope those motherfuckers die." The substitute teacher seemed a little confused then grinned. Someone had overheard her in the parking lot calling her boyfriend a motherfucker. There were eight weeks of 10th grade left.

Ellen raised her hand. Usually she never spoke in class but no one was paying attention today. A group of kids were playing a board game on four desks pushed together. "We should use nonviolence," she said.

"I hope those motherfuckers get really fair trials so they get what they deserve and die."

"I guess," Ellen said. She wasn't sure. Didn't the terrorists just want to be happy like everyone else? When people ate at McDonald's weren't they killing people—by supporting McDonald's and enabling it to open more restaurants in places like Japan, where the kids would then grow up fat and diseased and get heart attacks or cancer and die—just like terrorists? Weren't the terrorists at least less circuitous, a little more honest? Why didn't the news care that much when all those Africans killed each other in Rwanda? Why didn't McDonald's open free restaurants in Africa and save people? Why was the teacher letting everyone say 'motherfucker'?

"What is the theme of *1984*?" said the teacher. They were discussing *1984*.

Ellen raised her hand. "I think it talks about how the government can trick us and control us. Like they're doing right now.

Because they're making us think that American lives are worth more than British lives and that British lives are worth more than African lives." She blushed.

The teacher nodded a little. She picked up the yardstick and pointed it at someone, who looked blankly at her.

"In the end they play chess," someone else said. "After they use the rat on him they play chess."

"Chess is boring," said the teacher. "Does anyone else think chess is boring?" She was just out of graduate school, and she didn't care. In the parking lot she had called her boyfriend a 'motherfucker.'

"People who play chess could be spending their time growing tomatoes in their backyard," Ellen said. "Remember the news this morning when they said that two people in London died? If I did the news, I'd say that people who play chess killed five hundred people in Africa because of being apathetic and not helping with their own gardens. That's true. That's a fact." She did not want to argue with anyone. She was just saying things that were true.

"I think if they make the movie—*1984*, the movie—I think everyone should have long hair and listen to heavy metal," said the substitute teacher. "And wear those dyed shirts and have holes in their jeans and sit around watching *The Breakfast Club*."

A few kids laughed, and then Ellen raised her hand. "Why are you acting like that?" she said.

"Like what?" said the substitute teacher.

"I don't know," Ellen said.

"Speak to me after class," said the substitute teacher, then drew a caricature of George Orwell on the blackboard. It was pretty good, but the class had lost interest in her, and began to talk to each other about *Family Guy*, online role-playing games, and how it would be fun to wear football helmets and light fireworks and then hit the fireworks back and forth with tennis rackets at each other's heads. "If I don't do that tonight I'm beheading myself looking in the bathroom mirror," someone said.

"What's your name?" said the substitute teacher after class to Ellen.

"I don't know," Ellen said.

The teacher laughed. She didn't stop. It seemed like she didn't stop. Ellen walked out of the classroom. In her next class she drew a picture of a Native American leading an army of turkeys to the White House. The turkeys looked like cupcakes. She drew arrows at the turkeys and wrote, "Turkeys." After class, a girl wearing a shirt that said "Mineral" approached her. "Hey," she said. "I like what you drew." Ellen blushed. "Did you tell that substitute you didn't know what your name was? That's good." Ellen didn't know what to say. She never knew what to say. "I hate school," she said. A group of kids walked by and the girl with the "Mineral" shirt went with them. Ellen sat through three more classes. After school she wanted to smash things. She walked home, across a field and a street. At home she sat on her bed. Sometimes she sat thinking, "Ellen... Ellen... Ellen... Ellen...

Ellen..." and she did that now. She thought about dying. After a while she lay down. She felt hungry. She stood and a dolphin was there.

The dolphin quietly went, "Eeeee eee eeee."

"Do you want to play with me?" the dolphin said.

Ellen looked at her feet. "Okay," she said.

The dolphin held Ellen's hand.

They went in the backyard and the dolphin opened a trapdoor.

They climbed down a ladder.

Halfway down a bear was coming up.

"Use teleport," the dolphin said.

"I don't have it," the bear said.

"Why not?"

"I just don't," the bear said.

"Are you sure?"

"Oh yeah. Wait. I forgot that I had the ability to teleport," the bear said.

"A sarcastic bear," the dolphin said.

"A bear. A sarcastic bear. A bear, a dolphin," the bear said. "A stupid bear. A fucking moose."

"We have two people so you go down," the dolphin said.

"Fine," the bear said. "Life is stupid anyway."

The dolphin and Ellen and the bear went down the ladder.

There was a corridor.

"Thank you," the dolphin said to Ellen.

The dolphin hugged Ellen.

"I like you," the dolphin said.

The dolphin looked at Ellen.

The bear scratched the wall a little.

"Thank you for coming, Ellen," the dolphin said.

Ellen looked at her feet.

She had plastic sandals.

The sandals were green and blue.

The bear made a quiet high-pitched noise.

Ellen made eye contact with the bear.

"Do you want to come?" Ellen said to the bear.

The bear scratched the wall and looked at the dolphin.

"No," the bear said. "I wouldn't have fun anyway. I can't have fun in groups of three."

The bear knelt and opened a trapdoor and tried to crawl in but didn't fit.

The bear stood.

"I don't need to go there," the bear said.

The bear had a blanket and it folded it neatly.

"I don't know," the bear said. "I'll go work on my novel I guess."

The bear went up the ladder.

The dolphin and Ellen walked to a cliff.

The dolphin knelt and opened a trapdoor.

They crawled through a tunnel.

There was a room.

It had a bed, a refrigerator, a Christmas tree.

The Christmas tree had blinking lights.

"Are you hungry?" the dolphin said.

The dolphin gave Ellen a muffin on a plate.

"A little," Ellen said.

The dolphin watched Ellen eat the muffin.

"Thank you," Ellen said.

"Do you want cake?" the dolphin said.

"I don't know," Ellen said.

The air conditioner went off.

The room was very quiet.

The Christmas lights blinked.

The refrigerator was very quiet.

"Do you want to come over again?" the dolphin said.

"Okay."

The dolphin held Ellen's hand and they went to Ellen's room.

"I had a lot of fun," the dolphin said.

Ellen hugged the dolphin.

The dolphin cried.

The dolphin very quietly went, "Eeeee eee eeee."

"You are nice," Ellen said.

"Did you like the muffin?" the dolphin said.

"Yes," Ellen said.

The dolphin looked at Ellen.

Ellen sat on her bed and looked at her hands.

Ellen looked at her sandals.

The dolphin looked at Ellen's sandals.

"Do you want to do something else?' the dolphin said.

"Okay."

The dolphin held Ellen's hand.

They went through the trapdoor and the corridor down a ladder into an elevator.

The elevator had mirrors.

Ellen looked at herself and the dolphin.

The dolphin was smoother.

The dolphin put a blindfold on Ellen.

They walked across a rope bridge and Ellen heard hamster noises.

The dolphin took the blindfold off Ellen.

They crawled through a tunnel.

There was a playground.

Ellen walked into the playground and felt very quiet.

She felt very calm.

The dolphin went down the slide.

Ellen climbed onto the slide and went down the slide.

The dolphin went, "EEEEE EEE EEEE."

Ellen went to the swings.

The dolphin and Ellen did the swings.

"EEEEE EEE EEEE," went the dolphin.

Ellen looked at the dolphin's face.

The dolphin's face looked handsome.

Ellen looked at the dolphin going, "EEEEE EEE EEEE."

Dolphins felt top-heavy, that year, most of the time, and wanted to lie down. When their heads weren't on top they still felt top-heavy, but metaphysically. In public places they felt sad. They went into restrooms, hugged themselves, and quietly went, "Eeeee eee eeee." Weekends they went to playgrounds alone. They sat in the top of slides—the enclosed part, where it glowed a little because of the colored plastic—and felt very alert and awake but also very sad and immature. Sometimes they fell asleep and a boy's mother would prod the dolphin with a broom and the dolphin would go down the slide while still asleep. At the bottom they would feel ashamed and go home and lie in bed. They felt so sad that they believed a little that it was their year to be sad, which made them feel better in a devastated, hollowed-out way. Life was too sad and it was beautiful to really feel it for once; to be allowed to feel it, for one year. When dolphins had these thoughts, usually on weekends at night, it was like dreaming, like a pink flower in a soft breeze on a field was lightly dreaming them. The sadness was like a pink forest that got less dense as you went in and then changed into a field, which the dolphins walked into alone. Sometimes the sadness was like a knife against the face. It made the dolphins cry and not want to move. But sometimes a young dolphin would feel very lonely and ugly and it was beautiful how alone it felt, and it would become restless with how perfect and elegant

its sadness was and go away for a long time
and then return and sit in its room and feel
very alone and beautiful.

Sometimes when dolphins went to playgrounds alone they did the monkeybars and
went to the swings and on the swings thought,
"I hate this stupid world."

They thought, "I hate it."

They cried a little with the wind against
their face.

They felt so bad that they went away.

And found Elijah Wood and told Elijah
Wood to go with them and Elijah Wood
went—because he thought it was a movie.
Elijah Wood and other celebrities like Salman
Rushdie rode dolphins in rivers. Salman
Rushdie felt proud and famous. And the dolphins swam to islands and beat Elijah Wood
and the other famous people with heavy
branches. They cried when they murdered
human beings, and it was terrible.

One dolphin had a battle axe and killed
Wong Kar-Wai.

Wong Kar-Wai was easier because he wore sunglasses and couldn't really see the terror.

Sometimes dolphins knew other dolphins—cousins, uncles—that had died, and they said, "It is sad they died but there is nothing to do except be nice to anyone still alive." But they themselves had not been nice. They had killed Elijah Wood, Kate Braverman, and Philip Roth—people like that. They had made promises and forgotten. One dolphin had become friends with a man with Down syndrome and the man had written the dolphin a letter and the dolphin had not responded. Another dolphin had made promises to meet a person—had promised, and promised again, a third time—and had not kept them, and it had hurt the person.

And so they said, "I need to be nicer from now on," and went home.

At home they decorated their Christmas trees and sat on the floor.

"I have no one to be nice to," they thought.

They went to an acquaintance's home—to try to be friendly and compassionate to someone—but were not invited inside, and went back home, and thought about how as a young dolphin they had thought that the Gulf War happened in the Gulf of Mexico.

"Do you want to see an independent movie?" Jan said in the car. She reached over and patted Ellen, her daughter, on the head. They were driving somewhere. Ellen had been sitting there, on the sofa, drinking water; her mom had said something about Vitamin D, or something; and now they were going someplace. It was Spring Break for Ellen. So far she had drank water on the sofa while thinking about how to destroy the local Starbucks; ate a bag of carrot sticks while walking around the neighborhood, feeling afraid of people; and, the day before that, slept sixteen hours. A few more days and she would be sitting there again, in Advanced Placement American History. Her teacher, who was also the football coach, would make fun of Sacco and Vanzetti. People would take notes. *Sacco and Vanzetti are pansies.*

Ellen didn't respond so Jan patted her again; and kept patting and then patted Ellen's forehead a little too.

"You're going to crash!" Ellen said. She didn't trust her mom. But she shouldn't be afraid of dying, she knew. It would happen, of course. "It's okay if you crash. I'm just saying. You might."

"You like independent movies because they are real. They have meaning. Those movies where things keep changing. Mutants," Jan said carefully. "People don't change like that. They don't fly and shoot lasers from their eyes. That's not real."

"You don't know what you're talking about. It's about how controlled by money things are, not how real."

"We'll adopt a lot of dogs for free," Jan said. "Is that what you mean?"

Ellen was confused a little. "Maybe. But people are always like, 'Plants are alive too, and you eat those, hypocrite.' But what's worse? Murdering a thing with nerves and a nervous system or murdering a thing that only might have those? I mean, people are stupid."

"Tomorrow we'll adopt one dog," Jan said. "We'll do it at night, and we'll ride bikes so we don't waste gas. Do you like that? Adopting dogs at night, doesn't that sound fun? What will we name them? I said one. We'll get two."

"I'm serious," Ellen said.

"What's your favorite animal?" Jan said.

"I don't know," Ellen said without thinking.

"Is it a horseshoe crab?"

"I don't know," Ellen said.

There was a store outside, passing by, where they sold hunting gear. It had a canoe glued on its front. Who needed to murder a deer then sit in a tree and float down a river? "I'm going to kill everyone," Ellen said. She was against violence, she knew.

Jan smiled at her daughter. She moved her hand to pat Ellen's head then stopped, half-way, and pulled her arm back.

"Everyone should be impeached," Ellen said. "For being so bad at living." What happened if an unemployed person was laid off? Ellen's mind went blank. She wanted to swim with young dolphins in a small, clean, shallow ocean—with that silky kind of sand that didn't have any shells in it. Was that what she wanted? She wasn't a good swimmer.

"Impeachment," Jan said. "Is that a euphemism? Yeah. That's what they do. Make everything sound nice, like life's just eating peaches all day. That's nice of them. Optimistic."

"Anything in the world is a euphemism," Ellen said. "There's just one thing to life. It's just this... thing. Everything else is just a euphemism for the thing. The oneness. I know what I'm talking about." Ellen felt a prickling sensation on the top of her head. The cloth—or whatever—ceiling of the Buick was hanging down on her hair, like a skullcap. "It's all atoms, right? So everything's just the same. I mean, without perception there's just... a nothing-thing. It's just one thing. Whenever you talk or use your senses you're distorting that thing, trying to make it into a lot of different things—like trying to separate it from what it really is. I'm not the only person who says this. Buddhism does, and other people. I'm not stupid."

"Your little sisters are... do you think they are a little strange?" Jan said loudly.

"Strange people are better," Ellen said.

"Your brother Steve is not strange," Jan said.

"I don't care. I mean... he's older."

"I'm stopping at the grocery," Jan said. "You want to wait in the car? Come in with me—it'll be fun."

"What? How is being a consumer fun?" But people had to eat, Ellen knew. Buying food was okay, wasn't it? Just enough to survive. Nothing more. "We should grow our own food."

"Should we grow food for the dog that we'll adopt tomorrow?"

"Don't try to change me. A dog isn't going to change me."

"Maybe we should wait until after Thanksgiving for the dog. Thanksgiving is so soon! Aren't you excited?"

"I hate all holidays." Thanksgiving—the gorging and genocide of it; how could it be a holiday? were they serious?—made Ellen feel at once nauseous, sarcastic, seditious, and starving. Her mouth watered. But she also wanted to vomit on the white man's face then smash something—a house, an entire mansion—with her forehead and have it be suicide at the same time.

"When you were a kid... I remember your face on Christmas. Smiling, bright. Remember you made those lists for me? It would have these little things you wanted. It would be numbered. Like *one*, a stuffed animal, *two*, whatever... then there would be a few numbers where you wrote 'mystery thing,' 'mystery thing,' 'mystery thing.' You wanted to be surprised."

She was so superficial and materialistic back then. She was stupid. She was someone else back then. "That's wasn't me. I mean, I can't be held accountable for anything I've done in the past," Ellen said. She was startled a little. Was this true? "Each moment... is just a moment. Time is like, a thing. And space is another thing. You wouldn't say I'm responsible for things occupying other spaces, like everyone killing everyone else in wars or beating a wife. So you shouldn't say I'm responsible for things that occupy other areas of time." She was excited. It made sense. She felt like she could do things now. Play and be wild and not have to be afraid or nervous anymore. Then the feeling passed. She could do nothing. She couldn't play with anyone. The feeling always passed.

"You were always smart. Smarter than me. As smart as your dad. You used to sit there and say, 'Tell me to multiply 40 and 25.' And then you'd say the answer. I always told you that you would be good at anything you worked at." Jan looked at Ellen a moment. "Um," she said. "Don't be mad when I say this. But... it's not too late to restart piano lessons."

"Playing piano and being politically apathetic are the same thing," Ellen said, a bit rotely, as if she'd said it before, though she couldn't be sure if she had.

A Honda Civic with at least four bears inside passed Jan's car.

A bear was on top of the car, stomach down.

Jan pointed at that.

They stopped at a stoplight and waited and continued driving.

"When I'm old I want to live in a cabin on the beach," Jan said. "I'll wake up, eat fruit, play the piano. I think I'll take a nap and read a book. That's what I'll do. I'll be playing the piano and I'll think, 'I think I'll nap and read,' then I'll go do it. Doesn't that sound so nice?" Jan made a sudden U-turn. A couple of cars honked. She parked in front of a Wal-Mart grocery store. There was a tired look on her face as she slowed the car to get it just right.

It took a long time to make the car go from fast to slow to stop, Ellen felt. It was hard to slow to a stop. Ellen felt nervous, because of how strange it was to slow down, how terrible it must be for Jan to have the responsibility of carefully slowing the car to a stop without crashing. Then Ellen felt normal again. They were just parking the car. The car was still moving. Ellen looked at her mom, who was trying to park the car. A person, Ellen thought, and felt sad. Inside, putting peaches into a plastic bag, Jan said she was flying to Las Vegas to gamble for a few days. Ellen asked if she could go. Jan told Ellen to go get a package of salmon. Ellen went and got an organic avocado and thought about gambling and brought back the avocado. Jan said she knew Ellen would get something else—not a salmon. Ellen said gambling was good because it kept people inside, where they couldn't hurt anyone, and where they could get rid of their extra money, but bad because it increased the divide between the rich and the poor. Jan said she would donate her house to the poor, and they would all live in a forest, with dogs. Ellen said she wished that would happen. Jan pointed at something and said, "Look at that organic fruit." Ellen looked. Jan quickly walked to and hugged her daughter.

A few weeks passed and Ellen didn't make any friends—she talked once to the girl with the "Mineral" shirt but then didn't see her again—and then 10th grade was over and it was summer. Ellen's mom, Jan, was going to Hawaii. She and her sister had planned to go to Las Vegas but then chose Hawaii, as a sort of joke, just to do it—vacation in Hawaii; why not?—and now the plane was about to crash. There had been an explosion or something. Jan and her sister were hugging. A flight attendant was telling everyone to hold themselves and lean forward into their laps and everyone did that and Jan's sister did it, and then Jan did it.

Everything was shaking and Jan was crying a little.

She thought of her daughters and Steve and saw some of their heads and faces in different angles, sort of floating around. She hugged her sister, who was in a kind of fetal position, and felt her sister's spine against her cheek and looked sideways out the window—something was flashing and behind that it was a very light blue, like a black that went past into white and then a little into blue—and thought that if she concentrated hard and moved very fast she could jump out of the plane and parachute onto a cruise ship that would be there, but that seemed too difficult, because she didn't have a parachute. It was very noisy and everything was shaking. Jan felt a little sleepy. She thought she should probably stay awake, to see what would happen, but she wasn't sure—it felt dangerous to know what was going to happen;

safer to just let it happen, outside of herself, like someone else's responsibility—and then the plane went into the ocean. But a few weeks before that, in July, Ellen had received forty posters in the mail; the package had said, "The United States Government." Ellen wasn't sure if they were allowed to do that—use tax-payer money on this. "Paste them in conspicuous areas around the city," said a pamphlet. She sat on the floor of her room, felt sad, and flattened out a poster in front of her. The poster had a handsome dragon. They were posters for the movie the president had written, directed, and starred-in.

"Why are you doing that?" said Ellen's brother Steve.

"I'm not," Ellen said. "Go away." She stared at the carpet.

"You go away. I own this room. I bought it from a government auction with fake bids."

Ellen pushed Steve out of her room. While being pushed into the hallway Steve said, "I'm going to come in here tonight and superglue those posters to each of your clothes. Don't cry when it happens." Steve went to his room. He thought briefly about his life, felt a vague foreboding, and sat at his computer. He instant messaged Andrew, his acquaintance from high school who had gone to college in New York five years ago. Andrew worked in a library.

"Andrew," Steve typed in AOL instant messenger.

"Steve," Andrew typed.

"Karl's away message is 'Rock!'" Steve typed.

"I want to throw eggs at Karl's house," Andrew typed.

"I'm so hungry. I'm going to check the fridge." Steve sat there. He wasn't hungry. Maybe he was a little hungry. He couldn't tell. "We have six limes," Steve typed a few seconds later. He felt impatient.

"Make a line of subs. A subline," Andrew typed. Good one, Steve thought. It didn't make sense. In high school they did Sublime covers in Andrew's room. Maybe that was it. "We should just go assault Karl," Andrew typed. "We should break his leg."

"Ahahahahaah," Steve typed, and stared at his computer screen.

"Eggs aren't enough anymore," Andrew typed. "We will murder him."

"What about when he fell on the curb and broke his leg," Steve typed. "He said he was going to sue the government. For making the sidewalk slippery."

"I don't remember that," Andrew typed. "I can't remember anything anymore."

"Karl's buddy icon is a guitar. Douche bag."

"I have to go," Andrew typed. "My boss just walked by grinning. 'Passive-aggressive.'"

Steve lived in Orlando, Florida. His mom, Jan, was always at her sister's place—or wherever—playing Texas Hold 'Em, a kind of poker. She was going to Las Vegas soon, with her sister. Steve was twenty-four. He did not have a job. But he pretty much was raising Ellen and his other two sisters, who were seven and five or something. It was summer now so none of them had school except Ellen, who for some reason was taking summer classes—probably to try and make friends, Steve thought,

which made him feel empathy. Most nights
Steve and the people he went to high school
with played video games or drank beer while
playing poker; the same things they'd been
doing for about seven years, and the future—
or, rather, the past of some future's future,
Steve thought suddenly—was just another thing
that wanted to get away from everything else
and finally be completed, which is to say that
Steve himself had no future. The future was
only itself, and it didn't care; it was somewhere
else and it was already done, like bread in an
oven. Steve felt very calm. He moved icons
around on his computer for almost ten minutes,
drew five whales with Microsoft Paint, closed
the file without saving, went in the bathroom,
washed his hands, smiled exaggeratedly at his
own face for fifteen seconds and then watched
a movie he'd already seen, ate something without paying attention to what it was, went to
sleep, woke in the morning, made eggs for the
kids—six in one skillet; he would email
Andrew, he thought: "I cooked twelve eggs in
one skillet and it looked like a cake"—played

video games at a friend's house, came home, made dinner for the kids, watched TV, went in the bathroom, saw Ellen staring at her own face in the mirror, made eye contact with Ellen in the mirror, turned around to give Ellen privacy, felt Ellen walk quickly past him, into the hallway, and heard Ellen's door slam shut. He went into the bathroom, brushed his teeth, and flossed. He walked into the living room and saw his mom, Jan, on the phone. Jan stood and walked away into the computer room. Steve sat on the sofa. Ellen walked through the living room. She went into the computer room. She came out of the computer room.

"I'm bored," Steve said. "Where are you going?"

Ellen went in the kitchen.

Steve stood and went in the kitchen.

"Cook me a seven-course meal," Steve said. "Or I'll kill you."

"Go away," Ellen said. She walked into the living room.

Steve followed and pushed her from behind.

"You're in my way," Steve said.

Jan came out of the computer room holding the phone in front of her.

"It's for you," she said.

"Who?" Steve said.

"Both."

Steve took the phone. "Hello?" he said.

Ellen turned around a little. She walked toward a plant and looked at it. A plant. She walked vaguely in some other direction.

"Steve," Steve's dad said on the phone.

"Hi," Steve said.

"Your mother said you're all coming to visit me," Steve's dad said. "All five."

"You should visit us," Steve said.

"No," Jan said. "He won't leave."

"Yeah he will," Steve said into the phone and at his mom. "You can make him leave."

"Where is Ellen?" Steve's dad said.

Ellen was lying on the sofa facing the back of it. Her nose, eyes, mouth, and forehead were smushed into the sofa. Steve quickly walked there and sat on her. "I'm sitting on her," he said.

"Don't sit on your sister," Steve's dad said.

"She likes it," Steve said.

Ellen squirmed a little.

"She likes animals," Jan said.

"She likes everything," Steve said.

In middle school Andrew's World Cultures teacher, who smoked marijuana and always talked about taking the class on a field trip to Costa Rica, which everyone knew would never happen, had a party at her house and Andrew stepped on a window and broke it, then climbed through the glassless window to the back porch, where he and a friend, who Andrew, years later, living in Florida in his parent's house—working as a pizza delivery man and obsessed, in a half-hearted way, with a girl from two years ago—never saw or thought about anymore, took cans of soda and threw them over the backyard fence, into a retention pond, or something. It was very dark out. Then someone—maybe Andrew—thought it would be fun to throw the cans over the house itself, to the front yard, so Andrew did that and hit a girl named Patricia in the leg. Andrew went to the front yard. Patricia was crying. Girls began to crowd around her. The small crowd of girls went into an SUV and the SUV left like an ambulance.

When Andrew was seventeen Steve came over with other kids. They played video games and poker. Andrew's parents were not home. Andrew and Steve played drums and guitar until morning then went to school. Andrew drove. Steve was on his cell phone. While making a right turn Andrew put his head out the window and screamed "Shit" at a person in a car parked at a red light. Steve laughed and said into his phone that Andrew just screamed "Shit" at someone.

In college Andrew spent a few years not really doing anything or having regular friends.

He had a girlfriend for about a year and a half.

He wrote a novel. He met Sara.

They went to the grocery store.

She went to Florida with Andrew.

After a while she stopped talking to Andrew.

Andrew lived in Jersey City for a year.

One Saturday night it was snowing.

He was walking home.

The snow made the street very bright.

It was very quiet and late and very bright and Andrew felt strange.

In his room he sat on the floor.

He went to a Parisian-style café. He bought mashed potatoes and ice cream. It was very expensive. Andrew gave a twenty-dollar bill and the person said, "Do you want change?" Andrew hesitated and said "No." In his room he ate the food on the floor. There was an enjoyment to being alive, he felt, that because of an underlying meaninglessness—like how a person alone for too long cannot feel comfortable when with others; cannot neglect that underlying the feeling of belongingness is the certainty, really, of loneliness, and nothingness; and so experiences life in that hurried, worthless way one experiences a mistake (though probably the awareness itself, of nothingness, was the only mistake; some failure of optimism or illusion, to be corrected, somehow)—he could no longer get at. He felt very strange. It was late and there was nothing to do. He had no Internet and lived in New Jersey.

He went to the refrigerator and drank his housemate's wine coolers.

He did not know the housemate.

She lived upstairs.

They met in the kitchen once and the housemate's mother was there.

Andrew shook hands with the housemate's mother.

One weekend Andrew read *Chilly Scenes of Winter* by Ann Beattie.

He read half Friday night and half Saturday afternoon and it made him happy.

At night he showered.

He brushed his teeth in the shower.

He sat on the carpet.

He didn't have a chair.

Something fell on him.

He put his hand on his back and felt something.

Then saw a millipede running away very fast under the bed.

He looked at the ceiling and felt afraid and went to sleep.

One Friday he lay on his back on the carpet.

His computer was on the floor.

He listened to songs off his computer.

He listened to a song he had recorded one summer alone in his room in Florida.

He listened to it repeatedly then listened to other songs repeatedly.

In the morning he was standing in the bathroom.

He looked out his window.

A cat was staring at him.

The cat averted its eyes.

Andrew knew of Mark from a mutual acquaintance. They saw each other on campus one day and Andrew walked to Mark and they talked. They began to meet sometimes, to complain about life mostly. They usually met at night. Andrew told Mark that Fernando Pessoa was severely disillusioned but probably not always very depressed, because his thoughts were more exciting to him than anyone else's; and he understood the smallness and uselessness of a human life, did not believe in such a thing as 'sincerity,' and knew the possibility of a maid breaking a cup as the cup using the maid to commit suicide. Andrew told Mark to read *The Book of Disquiet*. Andrew said he had read all of Pessoa. Mark said he probably shouldn't read that book. They went to readings, including one where Andrew read poems he'd written about how he felt. ("It's just how I feel," he'd told his creative writing class, Freshman year, when asked what his poems— half-page things that looked legitimate from a distance; though what, from a distance, didn't?—were about.) They saw the new Batman movie and a week later Mark e-mailed Andrew and said there was a free concert in Battery Park. Andrew said he'd go. Andrew went. Yo La Tengo was supposedly playing. On the way Andrew began to make jokes about Yo La Tengo. "I feel like they're not from Mexico, but New Mexico," Andrew said. "I feel like they're forcing me to exploit migrant farmhands somehow." He went on like that for three blocks. "I can't listen to any band associated with The Flaming Lips or The Shins," he said, and pointed at people across the street who were wearing strange costumes, and asked if that was The Flaming Lips. Mark stopped walking. His face became indecisive. "Maybe I should go to this alone," he said. Andrew felt stupid. ("How do you have fun?") He didn't know what happened. He stopped making jokes and said he would walk there with Mark then leave—go to a bookstore.

"You're just going to complain the entire time," Mark said.

"I'm making jokes, not complaining," Andrew said.

"If you didn't want to come you should've just said so. I would've gone alone. I'm not...." He mumbled something.

"Um," Andrew said. "I wanted to come." He went to the bookstore and sat and read for two hours. He went to the café. He bought a muffin and ate it. He went to the poetry section and a hamster ran away around a corner.

Andrew walked around the corner.

The hamster was staring at Andrew.

"Come here," the hamster said.

Andrew went to it.

"Go here," the hamster said. It moved a little.

"Where?"

"Just look," the hamster said.

"I am."

The hamster was moving its arms a little. It pointed somewhere a little. "There," it said.

"Sorry," Andrew said. "I don't know where you're talking about."

"Wait," the hamster said.

But it went to leave.

"Sorry," Andrew said at it.

The hamster turned around.

It had very tiny arms.

"Try something else," Andrew said. "Can you point by headbutting?"

They went back to where they were before.

"Okay," the hamster said. "Go here." It walked carefully into a wall.

Andrew kneeled and touched where the hamster headbutted.

"It's a secret passageway," the hamster said. "Push it."

Andrew pushed the wall.

"Wait," the hamster said. It looked around. "Wait. I'm lost."

"Just tell me what it is."

"Wait," the hamster said.

"Just tell me something first," Andrew said.

"Fine," the hamster said. "But in the park."

They went to the park.

"Under the world there is a dolphin city," the hamster said carefully. "It isn't only dolphins. There are bears and moose."

"Bears and moose," Andrew said. "Do they fight?"

The hamster was on the bench. It had a neutral facial expression. Andrew stared at it. "Do they fight?" Andrew said after a minute. "Moose have antlers."

"I'm thinking," the hamster said. A few minutes passed.

"Just forget it," Andrew said. "It doesn't matter. They don't fight."

"No," the hamster said. "Just let me think for a minute. I have to walk to think." The hamster got off the bench and walked around on the ground.

A few more minutes passed.

The hamster climbed back on the bench and sat.

"There are hamsters," it said.

Andrew looked at it while it talked.

The hamster had a very neutral facial expression.

"Under the bear and dolphin city there is another metropolis," the hamster said very slowly. "A land of hamsters." A few minutes passed. "Hamsters are sad," the hamster said.

"Below the continent of hamsters... wait... I need to be careful. The dolphins are sad too. Below the hamsters..."

The hamster got off the bench and walked around.

"Are we friends?" the hamster said.

An owl came down and grabbed the hamster.

"Help," the hamster said.

Andrew stood.

The owl was gone.

The next day Andrew e-mailed Mark saying he was sorry he had ruined Mark's day. When he typed the email he felt sarcastic and bored. Sitting on the train later he thought, "I feel sarcastic and bored," though he did not. Mark did not respond, but a few weeks later flew back to Singapore, where he had been born 24 years earlier. Andrew's other acquaintance in New York City, Michael Fisher, e-mailed Andrew asking if Andrew wanted to see a movie. Andrew said yes, but an independent one. Michael was late. He said he was on the train and it stopped and they told everyone to get off. Andrew said he hated New York City. Michael said it was probably like this everywhere. Andrew said he had been to London and Taiwan and that their subway systems were both much better than New York City's. Michael said New York City's subway was older. Andrew said they were late for the movie. The theatre was small. There seemed to be no empty seats. The movie had started. "There's some in front," Andrew said. "I can't sit in the front," Michael said. Andrew looked at Michael. "I'll stand here. I'm fine," Michael said. "Oh," Andrew said. He went to the front and sat. He stared at the movie. There were days, recently, where he felt his inner-guide—himself, really; who was he kidding?—stop walking, sit down, stare abstractly into space for a very long time, laugh suddenly, stand up, clear its throat, affect seriousness and authority, look around, point in some vague direction, and continue onward. What did this mean? Maybe it was one of those things you ignored, like when couples fought in the streets. Andrew didn't know. He himself had once fought in the streets. On 10th Street or something he had sort of cornered his then-girlfriend, who was crying a little, against a fruit stand.

"Let's go somewhere else to do this," he said.

"You're embarrassed." She wasn't crying anymore, but looked a little bored. "Look at you, embarrassed."

"This is embarrassing," he said. "Yeah, I am embarrassed." Then felt good for being honest and agreeing for once, like a kind of grown-up—instead of automatically disagreeing in order to place himself in a position where he could prove himself right and some other person wrong—and wanted to console her (hug her, maybe; the fight was over) but instead stared at her. He didn't feel good anymore, only acutely and comprehensively unenthusiastic, as there was something joyless, unimaginative, and ultimately interminable about the truth. A world without right or wrong was a world that did not want itself, anything other than itself, or anything not those two things, but that still wanted something. A world without right or wrong invited you over, complained about you, and gave you cookies. *Don't leave*, it said, and gave you a vegan cookie. It avoided eye contact, but touched your knee sometimes. It was the world without right or wrong. It didn't have any meaning. It just wanted a little meaning.

"Can we stop standing here?" said Andrew's then-girlfriend. "Can we eat now?"

After fighting they would feel both ethereal and adamantine, like crystals—and legitimate, like after a good workout. They would relax a while. Put some fruit on a plate, eat two or three Kit-Kat bars, and, between shows on TV, then, with the TV still on—and the following being more the result of logistics and precondition (laying on the same twin-size bed) than lust, or love, or whatever—have an impersonal sort of sex. In class the next day, well rested and decently-caffeinated, they would sit there making what-if jokes. ("What if I brought a tent to class, and went inside it?") Evenings, they'd fight. ("You do your hair before seeing other people but not before seeing me, I noticed.") Weekends, one of them would suggest hanging out with friends and then on Sunday hate the other person for acting different around friends—"So you like *Catcher in The Rye* because you identity with everyone not Holden, right? I mean, I don't understand. You yourself act so fake"—and fight. It was not a bad life. It was a life hollow with too much affect from either extreme. It was like living inside a cave: things in the periphery always seemed a little phosphorescent; whenever anyone talked it echoed and sounded melodramatic; and somewhere nearby was a waterfall, the noise of which made it always feel like you'd just been tranquilized, tagged, and released—a wholesome, non-drowsy drowsy sort of feeling, not unlike being on Tylenol Cold.

But that was two years ago, junior year in college. Sometimes now Andrew would be on the train, reading selections from Schopenhauer (*Studies in Pessimism*—he shouldn't, he knew, no one should ever), or else sitting there, at one of his two jobs—at the IFC movie theatre on 3rd Street, or in NYU's library, by Washington

Square Park, checking his e-mail—and he'd catch himself thinking, "I don't know how to feel happy," or "I am fucked," or, more recently, "I ____ ____," like a Mad Libs, which was kind of hopeful, he guessed; not completely a bad sign. What frightened him (though sometimes calmed him) was the first of those thoughts, about not knowing how to be happy; there was something irreversible about it, except possibly by potion or true love, like in every movie by Disney, as it was like a fairy tale in that sketched-out, theoretical way. But it was a fairy tale gone wrong, without any domestic whimsy or fast-moving plot, and in real time, without any pleasant summations of long periods of despair, loneliness, and ennui. It just didn't seem good, or allowed. It felt off-limits, or something. Was this for real? Andrew had forgotten how to be happy! He suspected that it involved unwarranted feelings of fondness for other people, too much self-esteem, a sort of long-term delusion that manifested as charisma, and a blocking out of certain things, like lonely people, depressed people, desperate people, homeless people, people you've hurt, people you like who don't like you, politics, the nature of being and existence, the continent of Africa, the meat industry, McDonald's, MTV, Hollywood, and most or all of human history, especially anything having to do with the Western Hemisphere between 1400 and 1900, plus or minus 200 years—but he wasn't sure. Why did it involve so many things? Maybe it was just too hard. One time Andrew had wanted to go to a Rainer Maria concert, had ripped out and carried around for weeks the listing from the *Village Voice*; but the day of the show at work in the library, sitting there, staring across the study area at something inanimate yet somehow vaguely annoying—though what wasn't vaguely annoying, these days?—thinking about staring at the web page where he would have to click something to find out how to pay with his HSBC checking card, doing the e-mail confirmation, taking the train to Red Hook or wherever and asking and getting told the wrong directions and ending up under some highway overpass, feeling homeless and addicted to heroin, he'd thought, finally, then—with a strange, voice-over sort of detachment, as if viewing his own life on a movie screen, in an empty theater—"It's too hard." It had become an inside joke, but a private one (which complicated things in a bad way), for Andrew to wait until the last moment and then no matter how easy the task think, "It's too hard."

After the movie Andrew saw Michael sitting on a bench in the lobby reading the *New Yorker*.

"When did you come out?" Andrew said. Michael said about 15 minutes into the movie. He said he had felt nauseous, like he might vomit. Andrew said the movie was really good. Michael talked about the social conventions of vomiting in public. Andrew said he was going to the bookstore. Michael said he was sleepy and wanted to go home. He went home. Andrew knew that Michael hung out with other people in the city, but never invited Andrew. It was like Michael was keeping Andrew separate, which Andrew thought was funny.

On the Internet Andrew learned that
Michael was old—twenty-eight. Andrew was
twenty-two. They had gone to college together.
Michael must have not done anything for about
five years after high school. Andrew was
friends with Michael's roommate and Michael's
roommate said that Michael never talked about
his parents or past, usually he just sat at his
desk reading the newspaper. The next time they
met for a movie Michael was late again. He
told Andrew he had a problem with leaving his
apartment, that he would always be worried
about forgetting something—like turning the
oven off. "Obsessive compulsive," Andrew said.
"No, not really," Michael said. "Do you have
to turn on and off the lights five times, is it like
that?" Andrew said. Michael said he was thinking about becoming a pilot. Andrew said that
was scary. Michael said he liked to sit, so flying would be good. They watched *2046*, the
new Wong Kar-Wai film. Michael said it was
too long. Andrew said it was stupid—too stupid. Outside, Andrew dropped his cell phone.

The battery detached and bounced and a young lady almost fell. She picked up both parts of the phone and gave them to Andrew.

"I have her fingerprints," Andrew said to Michael. "I did that on purpose. Now I'll frame her for murder. I should do that."

Michael argued earnestly against that; said it would never work. Andrew said he would drop a gun one day and Michael would pick it up and his fingerprints would get on it. Michael said Andrew would go to jail. Andrew said he would bribe the judge. Michael argued against that. Andrew said he would hire someone to fly a helicopter into the prison to take him away— to Alaska. Andrew said he would hire Michael to do it, once he got his flying permit. Michael said he was going to the Prince Street station. Andrew said bye. They did not talk to each other after that, except occasionally through e-mail. Sometimes Michael would e-mail Andrew an online coupon for Border's bookstore.

One day Michael e-mailed Andrew saying he was giving up on his novel.

He had priorities in life and was getting old and did not have enough energy for the novel.

Andrew emailed back, "Hmm."

At the movie theatre where Andrew worked Andrew's manager said he was quitting. He said he was moving out of the city, to grow a garden. He gave Andrew a note that recommended Andrew take his place as manager. Andrew used the note and was promoted to manager. The manager that had quit then came back and was rehired. Then they decided there were too many managers, and Andrew was let go. This all happened in one week. On Sunday of that week Andrew went to a literary event and met Shawn, who referred Andrew for a job at the financial corporation he worked at. Andrew received an e-mail from the financial corporation asking for a cover letter, resume, and expository writing sample. Andrew e-mailed the financial corporation a blank document instead of his resume. He found out the day after. He e-mailed the financial corporation again and apologized and attached his resume, but it was a blank document again. Finally he e-mailed his resume and not a blank document, but it was in RTF, and wouldn't open for some reason. Then he e-mailed his resume as a Word document. The next day he went with Shawn to a book party for a young writer at a bar on Tenth Avenue. "I didn't know there was a tenth avenue," Andrew said. "There is no way I am going to enjoy myself at a book party in a bar on Tenth Avenue," Andrew thought. He stood in a corner and drank a free beer and talked to Shawn's friend Lelu, a photographer.

"How do you know Shawn?" Andrew said.

Lelu said they lived near each other, or something. They had seen each other across the street, through windows. She asked Andrew the same question. She was very tall—taller than Andrew.

"Why didn't you go to Shawn's reading Saturday?" Andrew said.

"I was in Washington, D.C."

"For what?"

Lelu said for a casting call. She said she wouldn't be chosen. She said it was in one room and all the girls were there and it was crowded and they were videotaped very quickly and that was it. Andrew for some reason thought they secretly filmed the girls while they interacted with one another naturally, and there was some miscommunication about that for a while. Finally Andrew understood that the girls had lined up against the wall, and sort of modeled—went in profile, turned around, etc.—and been taped a few minutes. Andrew said Lelu should be angry that she went just for that. Lelu said she was. Andrew said Lelu should have done something, like stolen something or destroyed something. "What did you do?" Andrew said. Lelu said she came back to New York. "Oh," Andrew said. Lelu asked Andrew about his own job prospects. Andrew said he had an interview but lied to the person and the person knew he lied. Andrew thought about admitting that he had just lied about that—he hadn't lied, actually, at the job interview—but then there was a small table that had no one there and Andrew and Lelu went and sat. Shawn came and grinned and asked if

Andrew was enjoying himself. Shawn introduced Andrew to someone. "He's in a band," Shawn said. Andrew shook hands with the person. There were three people in a row behind the person. Andrew asked Shawn who those people were. "Is that his band?" Andrew said. Shawn said they were his cousins from France, or something. Andrew nodded. Shawn left. Andrew grinned at Lelu. Lelu grinned at Andrew. Someone passed an art book—*Girls*—down the table. Lelu took it and looked at it. Andrew looked at Lelu looking at the art book called *Girls*. Someone introduced himself to Andrew and Lelu. He said he was also named Shawn—the book party was for a person named Shawn; the person who Andrew came here with was named Shawn—and had written a novel called *Girls*. He said he was writing a book called *Video Game Art*. He pointed at his editor and Andrew looked at the editor. Andrew said something about the title *Video Game Art*; he did not know what he was saying while saying it. Shawn talked about *Video Game Art*, his book, for five minutes without stopping. After one of those minutes Andrew stopped looking at Shawn's face and Shawn talked exclusively to Lelu. Lelu laughed and told some anecdotes. Andrew felt jealous that Lelu didn't tell those anecdotes to him. Shawn, author of *Girls* and *Video Game Art*, left. A dolphin came and introduced itself to Andrew and Lelu then spilled a green alcoholic drink on itself. The dolphin blushed. It took a smoke bomb and some matches out and dropped the smoke bomb before it was lit. The dolphin began very loudly to go, "EEEEE EEE EEEE." Someone punched the dolphin in its face and the dolphin fell. The same person picked up the dolphin and put it on a table by a window facing the street, then pushed the dolphin out the window while looking in the other direction. The other Shawn came and sat at the table Andrew was at and then a lot of other people came and sat and pulled up some more tables to create an enormous table, where everyone, including the young writer named Shawn, who the party was for, sat and looked at each other. Some talked to each other. Andrew was staring around, at the ceiling, mostly, when the young writer named Shawn loudly said Andrew's name and asked Andrew what he thought the apocalypse would be like. Andrew didn't know how the young writer who had written a book about rich, drug-addicted young people knew his name. Andrew said the train station under Union Square. Andrew cited the movie *Total Recall*. There was a silence. Andrew looked at the faces that were looking at him. Some people disagreed with Andrew. One person agreed. Andrew couldn't tell who; maybe the girl to his left. Andrew began to elaborate, citing how people in the Union Square station looked like mutants, like in *Total Recall*; also citing the sludge that was everywhere in the train station under Union Square; and the screeching noises. Then he interrupted himself in a louder voice and said that maybe the young writer should write a novel about the apocalypse. The young writer looked offended, or else bored; or, rather, Andrew felt that he had offended the young writer. Maybe the young writer had already written a book about the apocalypse.

Andrew felt embarrassed and slowly turned his head so that he was looking again at the ceiling. Lelu was still looking at the art book called *Girls*. Shawn stood and went outside to smoke. Lelu stood five minutes later and said she was leaving. Andrew stood and said he was also leaving. He didn't know anyone here. He thought about maybe stealing *Girls*, the art book. He and Lelu went outside. Shawn was smoking. Shawn said the word 'Networking' in a way that indicated at once his disdain, interest, and amusement with 'Networking.' Andrew said that the young writer whose book party this was for looked like a rock star. Lelu said she didn't think so. Andrew said a movie star. Lelu said she could see that. Shawn said the guy he introduced Andrew to who was in a band—that one time Shawn went to his apartment and saw a strange, metallic thing on a chair. It was three laptops stacked on top of one another. At the subway station the president came out. Shawn, Lelu, and Andrew were in a networking mood and it would be good to network with the president. They invited the president to eat sushi. At the sushi bar the president said it was stupid to be president.

"Power is stupid," the president said.

The president said he was an alien. He was from a different planet. He came here and was bored. "I felt I needed a goal," he said. "Now I'm the president. I have no human preconceptions, because I'm from a different galaxy. Listen to me, since I'm the ruler. You chose me. People need to process what I say. I'm the—I'm the fucking president. Patriotism is the belief that not all human lives are worth the same. Actually there is a oneness in the world because of consciousness and this oneness—what does it want, mostly. To avoid pain and suffering, seek pleasure and happiness. Patriotism and everything else like language denies the oneness; makes a twoness, threeness, so on. Why are we born? Why do we die? Where do we go when we die? Where did consciousness come from? Politics does not acknowledge those questions. Politics says, 'Have we blocked out enough information so that the word "progress" has meaning? How do we distract

from the mystery and oneness of existence?'
Politics is a pretend game where it is very
important to block out the information that it
is a pretend game. I'm the president, I think.
There is no good or bad. You arrive. Here you
are. No one tells you what to do. So you make
assumptions. Or you believe someone else's
assumption. A common assumption is that pain
and suffering is bad. But how do you know if
an action will increase or decrease net pain and
suffering in the universe from now until the end
of time? You can't know. Impossible. You
don't know if drawing your friend a picture
will or will not cause fifty thousand years of
suffering to ten million organisms on Alpha
Centauri one billion years from now. So you
create context. A common context is one's life
plus the next few generations, not including
animals, plants, or inanimate objects, and only
on Earth, with emphasis on one's own country.
So now you've made an assumption and also
blocked out more than 99.9% of the universe,
99.9% of all life on Earth, and an infinite or
unknown amount of time. You live a horribly

distorted life. You don't know anything. Fuck you if feel angry at someone else. I'll kill you. You are stupid and boring. Killing isn't bad. The only thing to be angry at is existence itself. We all force our assumptions and contexts onto other people. Each thought influences our actions and each action exists inside—and so influences—the world. That is politics. But who cares? How can you be angry at someone else's assumption or context that was as arbitrarily chosen or adopted as your own? If you unsarcastically feel anger at anything except everything it means your context does not include the information that assumptions have been made and contexts have been created; so anger is okay, I guess. But any unsarcastic thought or action is a horrible distortion. Anything is a horrible distortion. We need to stop breeding. There are assumptions and contexts and we go around pretending and playing games by overlapping our assumptions and contexts with others until there is no more time left. Death is the taking away of assumption and context. Consciousness is being forced to assume and then block out information in order to be conscious. I don't know how to think about that. Everything is preempted by the knowledge of death anyway. How do we stop death? How do we actualize the oneness of consciousness? I think we build robots. We fill the universe with microprocessors and match the expansion of the universe with the expansion of our microprocessors. We make the universe one unconscious mass, one computer program, one assumptionless thing whose context is everything. One lonely, meaningless robot programmed to not feel lonely or meaningless, or think or know anything. Thank you for listening to me. It doesn't matter. The noises coming out of my mouth are the result of the physical laws of the universe, probably, of cause and effect, of my choiceless birth, which itself was the effect of the beginning of the universe. I didn't choose for the universe to begin. I guess, to be practical, uh, distribution of wealth, uninhibited sharing of material possessions, debasement and de-evaluation of human power and authority. Wariness against any kind of progress that involves numbers. I don't know. Thank you. Good night."

"You just told us 'thank you' and 'good night,'" Shawn said. "Uh."

"Thank you," the president said.

"Don't you need bodyguards?" Andrew said.

"Bodyguards are stupid," the president said. "But yeah. They're coming. They missed the train."

The president's cell phone rang.

It was coconut noises.

Shawn looked at Andrew.

Andrew grinned.

"Coconuts," Andrew said.

"Or bowling," Lelu said.

"Now it sounds like bowling," Andrew said.

"Coconuts is better," Shawn said.

"Now it's coconuts again," Andrew said.

"We're in a sushi place," the president said into his phone.

Andrew went to the bathroom.

In the bathroom Andrew felt bored. He looked in the mirror and there he was.

Andrew left the bathroom.

There was a moose, a bear, a dolphin, and an alien standing around the president.

Andrew tried to not look at the alien.

He looked at the dolphin.

"I'm Andrew," he said.

Andrew put out a hand to shake hands.

The president slapped Andrew's hand away.

Andrew glared at the president a moment then grinned.

"They don't have names," the president said. "You don't have to introduce yourself."

The waitress asked if Andrew wanted ice water.

"Okay," Andrew said.

"You don't do that with bodyguards," the president said. "I'm annoyed. How stupid is that."

"Why did you become president if you think it's stupid," Shawn said.

"I don't know," the president said. "Life is meaningless. Everyone knows this. Look at Fernando Pessoa. He knew the most that life was meaningless. But he was always worrying about things. If life was really meaningless you wouldn't worry about things."

"You've read Fernando Pessoa?" Lelu said.

"You have?" Andrew said to Lelu.

"Yeah, you?"

"Yeah," Andrew said.

"You?" Andrew said to the dolphin.

"Yeah," the dolphin said.

"Have you?" Andrew said to Shawn.

"No," Shawn said. "Who is he?"

"A Portuguese author," the moose said.

The bear slapped the moose.

"Who hasn't read this person?" Shawn said loudly.

Everyone had read Fernando Pessoa.

"You should just leave," the president said to Shawn.

"I already ordered," Shawn said.

"Just leave money for what you ordered," the president said.

Shawn took out his wallet.

He only had a hundred dollar bill.

"Leave it," the president said. "Wait. Is that counterfeit money?"

"It's real," Shawn said.

The president took it and put it in his pocket.

"You can leave now," the president said. "You can go home now."

Shawn left.

"That was mean," Lelu said. "I bet we won't even talk about Fernando Pessoa."

"He probably believes the moon is really Australia and that they're talking about Australia when they talk about the moon hoax, which he believes in," the president said. "Which means he doesn't believe in Australia."

The alien sat where Shawn had been sitting, next to Andrew.

Andrew felt afraid.

He went to the bathroom.

When he came back the alien was still there.

Andrew thought about sitting somewhere else but saw the alien looking at him.

The alien was talking and it stared at Andrew a little then calmly averted its eyes as it kept talking.

Andrew sat in his seat next to the alien.

"Fernando Pessoa said he respected Buddhists and monks and whoever," the alien was saying, "because they tried to escape life, to not accept what was given us—this life, this stupid life." The alien had a British accent. "I'm from Wales," he said to Andrew.

Andrew tried to nod but his neck was tense and it trembled a little.

"Pessoa said art was fun and beautiful because it was useless and had no meaning," the alien said. "And that life is not fun because there is always a goal; you always need a goal each day. He admired Buddhists and monks but that is not art. Buddhists and monks have goals."

"You can't be aware of the meaninglessness of life and all that if you're a Buddhist monk," the bear said. "It's just stupid. Everything is stupid." The bear took out a blanket and put it on the moose's head.

"If art is fun and beautiful you can't say it's useless," the president said. "You're wrong."

"What do you think?" Andrew said to the dolphin.

Andrew liked the dolphin.

"I want to sit," the dolphin said.

Lelu stood. "You can sit," Lelu said.

"I want to sit down on a large soft sofa," the dolphin said.

"Oh," Lelu said, and sat.

"Pessoa talked about there being no escape," the bear said. "He was right. Buddhist monks do not escape. No one escapes. If there were an escape it would be an escape to another place that you would have the possibility to escape from, so the only possible escape is to be in the act of escaping. Therefore the only way to escape is to not escape. Talking about this is stupid. Escaping is not the same as having escaped. It's stupid."

The moose bumped into a table and knocked the table over.

"I know someone," the president said. "He emailed me and said he wanted to invent a suicide gun. A special gun that you wouldn't need to use your toes to kill yourself with. That's a good idea."

"I have two wishes left," the bear said.

"Don't waste it on a suicide gun," the president said.

"No," the bear said. "I don't care."

"Thank you," the president said.

The bear wished for a suicide gun.

A shotgun appeared on the table.

"It's just a shotgun," Andrew said. "That's not fair."

"We should have been more specific," the bear said.

"We should have thought about it first," the president said.

"It's our fault," the bear said.

"Can you wish me a Concorde Jet?" Lelu said.

"I wish Lelu had a Concorde Jet," the bear said.

"Thank you," Lelu said. "Where is it?"

"Probably outside."

Lelu went outside.

She came back. "It's there," she said. "I'm going to Easter Island."

She left.

She came back and sat.

"Just kidding," she said. "I don't know how to fly it."

"Sell it," the bear said.

"Too much work," Lelu said.

"You wasted my wish," the bear said.

"Sorry," Lelu said.

"No, I don't care," the bear said. "I was just saying a fact."

"What did you use your first wish on?" Andrew said.

"Teleport," the bear said. "Everyone gets teleport. It's stupid."

"I would get teleport," Andrew said.

"If you don't get teleport you get made fun of," the bear said.

"Yeah," Andrew said.

"You're stupid if you don't get teleport," the president said.

"You're stupid if you wish for a suicide gun and get a shotgun," the alien said.

The bear patted the alien's head.

Andrew felt afraid.

Their food came and they ate it.

They were all vegans.

"I shouldn't be president," the president said after they ate and drank alcohol. "Thank you. Good night. Australia."

They were drunk.

The bear was riding the moose.

The dolphin was lying on the floor in the corner.

It had sat then fallen and was now in the corner facing the corner.

The alien was standing in a dark doorway.

Andrew was eating green tea soy ice cream and feeling depressed.

He was looking at the dolphin.

Someone had rolled the dolphin into the corner

Lelu was sitting with a neutral facial expression.

The president was playing poker with Salman Rushdie.

Salman Rushdie had come.

"Poker is stupid and boring with two people," the president said.

"Baseball," Salman Rushdie said. "I'm obsessed with baseball."

"There's a kind of poker called baseball," the president said.

"I want a Fatwa," Lelu said.

Lelu sat on the table and looked down at Salman Rushdie.

"How do I get a Fatwa," Lelu said. "I want a Fatwa."

"You are stupid and boring," the president said to Lelu.

"You're just trying to provoke me," Lelu said.

"You are stupid and boring," the president said to Salman Rushdie.

"I am Salman Rushdie," Salman Rushdie said.

Andrew didn't want anyone to start talking to him.

He stood and went to the bathroom.

The alien was in the hallway where the bathroom was.

Andrew felt afraid and went back to his seat and sat.

The bear fell off the moose.

Before the bear hit the floor it disappeared and reappeared in Salman Rushdie's lap.

The bear put a blanket on Salman Rushdie's head.

One night working at the library Andrew took a two-hour break instead of a one-hour break. No one noticed. Andrew did it a few more times. The next week people ganged up on him and Andrew was fired and after a while he had no more money. On the plane back to Florida he thought about how he had no friends. He thought it woozily, with a vaguely bewildering, vaguely tiring sense of scale—a secondhand sort of epiphany, removed from its source, smudged, moved elsewhere, experienced now without clarity or context, therefore less insight, really, than mood swing—that the Earth was a rock; the sun a rock caught fire; and the life of a person something like a small-scale disaster, too small to examine and solve but not small enough to independently stop existing, and so left there in it's own little vanishing haze of light and doors and pretty faces;

all of which was true, of course; all of which was probably true. He closed his eyes and listened to the noise of the engine. He imagined the plane falling to the ground. There was an appropriate reaction, a certain melodrama of the face, something demented yet earnest in the arrangement of eyelids and lips, for people in planes that were falling—and Andrew didn't know it, and if he did he would feel as if acting while doing it. In Florida he lived with his parents. He got a job at Domino's Pizza. He had worked there before, one summer. In August his parents moved to Germany, where they were born. Andrew cried one night in his childhood bed when he thought about death. Then he played the drums and felt better. He was pretty good on the drums. He should start a band. His parents had no friends in America. They left Andrew the house and two elderly dogs. Andrew began to hang out with his high school friend Steve, who had three sisters, one named Ellen. Steve was funny. Steve's mother had recently died in a plane crash. Steve was unemployed. Andrew and Steve played poker with people they went to high school with. Sometimes they drove to Cape Canaveral and played blackjack and poker on casino boats. Sometimes Steve played guitar and Andrew played drums. It was cloudy in November and Andrew went to Steve's house. Steve was making spaghetti and cutting tomatoes and garlic. "I feel like me right now," Steve said. Andrew walked into the living room and looked through the sliding glass door. Ellen was in the backyard. She was walking and she fell and stood and saw Andrew looking at her. She stared at him. He felt strange and went to the kitchen, where Steve was at the stove. "Steve," he said. Steve turned and looked insane. Andrew laughed. "It looks like your face is dreaming me," he said. Steve was smiling and he kept smiling and Andrew felt horrible, then went into Ellen's room and lay on the bed.

He had never been in Ellen's room.

If she came in he would tell her he was afraid.

He felt a little lonely. He felt good.

It was November.

He pulled the blanket over his head and listened to Steve, in the kitchen, cleaning dishes, then microwaving something, then nothing for a while; and then the TV, making a cheering noise.

AVAILABLE FROM FROM TAO LIN

"A REVOLUTIONARY." —*THE STRANGER (SEATTLE)*

"Tao Lin writes from moods that less radical writers would let pass—from laziness, from vacancy, from boredom. And it turns out that his report from these places is moving and necessary, not to mention frequently hilarious."
—Miranda July, author of *No One Belongs Here More Than You*

"Prodigal, unpredictable." —*Paste Magazine*

"Stimulating and exciting....It doesn't often happen that a debuting writer displays not only irrepressible talent but also the ability to undermine the conventions of fiction and set off in new directions." —*The San Francisco Bay Guardian*

"[A] harsh and absurd new voice in writing. Employing Raymond Carver's poker face and Lydia Davis's bleak analytical mind, Lin renders ordinary—but tortured—landscapes of failed connections among families and lovers that will be familiar to anyone who has been unhappy." —*Time Out Chicago*

SHOPLIFTING FROM AMERICAN APPAREL • 978-1-933633-78-7 / 112PP / PAPER /
$13.00/ $16.00 CAN
EEEEE EEE EEEE • 9781933633251 / 224 PP / PAPER / $14.95/$18.00 CAN
BED • 9781933633268 / 280PP / PAPER / $14.95/$18.00 CAN
COGNITIVE-BEHAVIORAL THERAPY • 9781933633480 / 104PP / PAPER / $14.95/$18.00 CAN